Maggie

Brides of Montana

Book Four

Cheryl Wright

Maggie

Brides of Montana – Book Four

Copyright ©2022

by Cheryl Wright

Small Town Romance Publications

This is a work of fiction. Characters, places, and incidents are a figment of the author's imagination. Any resemblance to actual events, locales, organizations or people living or dead, is totally coincidental.

Dedication

To Margaret Tanner, my very dear friend and fellow author, for her enduring encouragement and friendship.

To Alan, my husband of over forty-nine years, who has been a relentless supporter of my writing and dreams for many years.

To You, my wonderful readers, who encourage me to continue writing these stories. It is such a joy knowing so many of you enjoy reading my stories as much as I love writing them for you.

Table of Contents

Chapter One

Shady Hollow, Montana – 1880's

Maggie Coulter clasped the bouquet she held, almost destroying the flowers with her tight grip. The exquisite handmade shoes she wore rubbed against her feet, and she wanted to kick them off. Her mother pulled the veil down over her daughter's face, and it instantly irritated Maggie's face. She blew at it, trying to move the unnecessary covering away.

"Honestly, Maggie," her mother said, frustration clear in her voice. "You only have to put up with it for ten minutes, maybe a little longer. Is it really that difficult?"

"Yes, Mother, it is. Why Marcus insisted on all this fanfare, I do not know." Why he insisted on marrying her was an even bigger question. She was quite happy spending time with him. The last thing Maggie wanted was to marry her childhood friend. To her, it was totally unnecessary. For Marcus, it was a whole different situation. He wanted heirs and wanted her to be the one to give them to him.

Before Marianne Coulter had the opportunity to answer, the organ music pealed out. "That's your cue, darling. Your father and I love you very much."

She straightened her daughter's veil, then focused on her husband's tie. "Hurry up, George," she said. "Don't keep Marcus waiting. You know how impatient he can be."

Maggie knew first hand how impatient Marcus was. He was a very caring man most of the time, but he was also incredibly impatient. She guessed it was because he was used to getting his own way.

Her father linked his arm through Maggie's, and they strolled down the aisle. Maggie's heart thudded in her chest. With each step she took, her misgivings grew stronger. She'd come this far, and knew she needed to follow through.

When the marriage was first suggested, she'd flinched. Every time he touched her or kissed her, she cringed. Not that Marcus was horrid, he wasn't, and in fact was the total opposite, but Maggie knew from the start he wasn't the man for her.

As her father handed Maggie over to Marcus, she felt faint. Surely all brides went through this very thing? She was startled by the preacher speaking. Marcus stared at her. "Are you all right, my darling?" he whispered as he patted her hand. It was all she could do to nod.

The words the preacher said all rolled into one and were virtually unrecognizable to her. Until he uttered the words, "Does anyone object to this man and this woman being joined in holy matrimony?"

Maggie suddenly lifted her skirts and shouted. "I do!" She ran down the aisle and out of the church. She could hear footsteps behind her.

"Maggie!" Her husband-to-be called out to her, but Maggie ignored him. She flicked the elaborate veil off her face and prayed for the wind to die down. She winced at the expense Marcus had gone to for this wedding, now wasted. Sure, he had the money, and she'd tried to tell him from the start she didn't return the love he declared for her, but he wouldn't have it. He was determined to make her his wife.

Maggie was certain she would be someone to provide heirs for him, and little more. Two highly regarded families brought together – that was the ultimate goal, she was confident.

She should have put her foot down from the start, but her mother was determined to see her spinster daughter married, not to mention her father. No one bothered to consider what Maggie might want. Her feelings, her aspirations, didn't come into it at all.

She jumped up into the buggy that was waiting for the happy couple. They were to leave for their honeymoon soon after the reception ended. Instead, Maggie would leave alone. As Marcus almost reached the buggy, she snatched up his bag and threw it at him. The surprised look on his face was priceless.

"Maggie, can we at least talk about this?"

He was right. They should discuss it, but it was too late. She'd made her decision, and there was no turning back. She urged the horse forward.

When she finally reached the outskirts of town, she dared to look back. Marcus was not there; he hadn't followed her as she'd expected. Not hoped, but expected. No one was there to convince her to return. Not a soul. *Did no one care she'd fled her own wedding?*

The *wedding of the decade* they'd called it. And now it was the disaster of the decade. Marcus was the richest cattleman in the county, and had pursued her for as long as Maggie could remember.

As she rode out of town, she'd planned to leave the buggy somewhere it could be easily found. She would unhitch the horse and ride to her destination.

Where that was, she had no idea. But she now realized if she did that, she would have nothing to her name. All her clothes and other belongings, things Marcus had purchased for her, especially for their honeymoon.

She stopped momentarily and removed the embellishments announcing they were *just married* – all added by family and friends.

Her eyes filled with tears. Did that make her a thief as well as a runaway bride?

Maggie traveled for what seemed an endless amount of time. She had a little money, as Marcus had afforded her an allowance since their engagement. It turned out to be a lifesaver.

Pawning her wedding dress for a little extra cash helped as well, although she knew she'd received less than half the value of the dress, but Maggie was grateful for the knowledge she had money for another night or two of food and board.

She ensured she had a hot meal at each town she stopped at, and availed herself of a warm bed, then left the next morning. Still not knowing where she headed, she urged the horse, a birthday gift from Marcus, to continue. She would know when she arrived that she'd reached her final destination.

Her future was now bleak, but with Marcus she had the promise of a secure home, a loving husband, and would never want for anything. It was a shame she didn't reciprocate his feelings, but Maggie had no intention of living the rest of her life in a loveless marriage.

They'd been friends since school, and although Maggie's family was not rich, they were well to-do and had good standing in the community. Both families always assumed the pair would marry. Too bad no one had consulted her.

Maggie lifted the reins and urged the mare forward. She could see the outline of a town in the distance, and was keen to get there before dark. Exhaustion threatened to overtake her. She didn't know how many days it was since she'd ruined her wedding, as the days all fell into one.

Finally arriving, Maggie found herself nodding off as she passed the sign announcing she'd arrived at Grand Falls. Expecting a dot of a town, she was surprised at the size of this place. Many of the buildings were new, which told her she was in the midst of a growing town. It was the sort of place she could meld into the background, a place she could hide without actually hiding.

She slowed her horse to glance about and liked what she saw. A large mercantile stood out amongst the other stores, as did the diner, butcher, and post office. A few people gathered along the boardwalk. A number glanced up and even waved at her.

Maggie had a good feeling about Grand Falls. She continued her perusal of the town, and would decide after a hot meal whether to stay or continue on to the next town. The draw of a hot bath, a warm bed, and a full belly decided for her.

"Welcome to Grand Falls." The older lady who served her at the diner, presumably the owner, sounded genuine. "Are you staying for long?" She handed Maggie a menu, and hovered, waiting for a response. "Allow me to introduce myself. Edna Baker, owner of this diner."

Maggie glanced up. Mrs. Baker seemed too old to be running a place like this alone. And she did appear to be doing it alone, as she couldn't see anyone else. "Thank you. Maggie O'…Coulter." She took a restorative breath. She had practiced called herself Mrs. Marcus O'Connor, all for nothing. "I've no idea how long I'll be here. Tonight at least." She smiled and was rewarded with a genuine smile from the elderly woman.

Suddenly Mrs. Baker glanced about and craned her neck to see outside. "Please tell me you didn't travel alone? Many a man has been attacked coming here across the plains. I can't imagine the danger for an unaccompanied woman." She frowned then, concerned for Maggie's safety.

Maggie's attention fell to her hands that sat in her lap. Mrs. Baker was right – it was sheer stupidity. Anything could have happened to her. Not that Marcus seemed concerned about her welfare. He hadn't even bothered to come after her. *Had she hoped deep down that he would? That he would convince her to marry him? Did Marcus have the same misgivings about their arranged marriage as she had?* She doubted that was the case. He had professed his undying love for her far too many times for that to be possible. *Or was it just a ruse?*

To get their families off his back? She would probably never know.

"I had little choice," she said, lifting her chin slightly, hoping the quivering was not noticeable. She had shed not a single tear over her wedding that had never eventuated.

"No choice?" Mrs. Baker pulled out a chair and sat beside her, reaching for Maggie's hands. "Are you in trouble, my dear?" Her voice was gentle and low.

Dragging courage from goodness knew where, Maggie turned to the woman and stared. "I'm a runaway bride. I had no choice but to travel alone."

The gasp from her companion was more than a little audible. It was clear for anyone to hear a few tables away. Luckily, Maggie was one of the few patrons in the diner. She was certain that wouldn't always be the case – the diner was quite large, with far more than a dozen tables set out.

"I apologize," Mrs. Baker said as she squeezed Maggie's hand. "I don't know what I expected you to say, but it wasn't that." She raised her eyebrows then, and Maggie knew this woman was a confidante for many of the women in Grand Falls. "Where are you staying? Not at that horrid saloon, I hope. It is the worst mistake this town made, allowing that monstrosity."

"Well, I considered it, but no. I have not yet found anywhere to stay. Is there a boarding house for women?"

"You look tired, my dear. Look over the menu and I'll get your meal sorted, then we can talk."

Maggie had an overwhelming feeling that Mrs. Baker would become her savior and lead her in the right direction. She glanced at the menu, glad for anything that would fill her empty stomach. Mrs. Baker took her order, then disappeared into the kitchen, appearing shortly afterwards with a steaming mug of coffee. Maggie had never felt more grateful, or more welcomed, for as long as she could remember.

"Now your belly is filled, and you are rested. What are your plans?" Mrs. Baker sat opposite Maggie, sipping on a coffee. She'd brought a fresh coffee for Maggie and a dessert of apple cobbler and clotted cream.

"I have no plans. I have been traveling all day, every day, moving from town to town, and not looking back."

"Oh my dear girl – you must be exhausted! The first thing we must do is secure a place for you to sleep." She glanced outside. "It's already dark. You'll stay with me tonight. Where is your horse? Already at the livery, I hope."

"Yes, she is already secured at the livery. And thank you for your kind offer, but I couldn't stay with you. It is such an imposition."

"It is far from an imposition. I get quite lonely living alone, and you need somewhere to sleep." She sipped her coffee again, then clapped her hands, startling Maggie, who was on the verge of falling asleep. "Finish your meal, and your coffee, and we will go. It's almost time for me to close up the diner, anyway."

She continued to sit at the table, then, without another word, headed toward the entrance to the diner and locked the door, preventing other would-be patrons from entering. Mrs. Baker then went into the kitchen. Maggie heard the clattering of pans and concluded the woman was washing dishes from her patronage tonight. Maggie wanted to help, but was far too exhausted to get up from her chair, let alone assist in the kitchen.

Before long, Mrs. Baker returned, and they were on their way to the older woman's home.

Maggie opened her eyes and glanced around. She should be used to waking up in strange places by now, but she wasn't. She knew she wasn't in a hotel, but her addled brain couldn't fathom where exactly she was.

That was, until her new friend, Edna Baker, tapped on the door. "Are you awake?" Not waiting for an answer, she entered the room, carrying a mug. "I thought you could do with a strong cup of coffee to wake you up. How are you feeling today?"

She sat on the edge of the bed holding the beverage while Maggie slid up the bed. "Good morning, and thank you," she said, still half asleep. "What time is it?"

"Nearly nine," Mrs. Baker told her.

Maggie sputtered at the revelation. "Please tell me you're kidding. I never sleep that late." She took the coffee handed to her and sipped it.

The older woman chucked. "Not kidding, but what does it matter? You obviously needed the sleep. From what you've told me, you've been on the move for days." Mrs. Baker considered her as Maggie sipped the hot beverage. "What are your plans? Will you stay a day or two longer?"

She came across as near desperate, and Maggie decided the woman was probably lonely. When they talked last night, Mrs. Baker explained she had lost her husband many years ago. She'd run the diner mostly by herself ever since, although she got help from time to time. Guilt kicked in, and the runaway bride felt obligated to her hostess.

"If it would help, I could stay on a day or two and assist you in the diner. It's the least I can do to repay your kindness." She studied Mrs. Baker as she considered the offer. "I can look for accommodation today, then…"

"My dear girl, you will stay here. I have no intention of kicking you out onto the street." Then she smiled. "I certainly would not deny your kind offer." She stood and began to turn away. "You can cook, can't you?" She shook her head then. "No matter. Serving tables would also be a great help."

"I can cook," Maggie said. "Mother said it was a skill I would never regret learning. Not that I've had a lot of practice, but I enjoy it."

"That's settled then. When you're ready, come out to the kitchen. Breakfast will be ready in a few minutes. We can talk more then." The broad smile on her face couldn't be missed. It warmed Maggie's heart to know she'd made the older lady happy, even if it was only for a day or two.

Chapter Two

After splashing cold water on her face, and tying her hair back, Maggie was ready to face the day. Breakfast was bacon and eggs with a side of toast and another mug of hot coffee. She and Mrs. Baker seemed to have an affinity with each other. They chatted as though they were old friends who were catching up after a period of not seeing each other. She felt very comfortable in the old lady's presence.

Once the dishes were washed and the kitchen tidied, they strolled toward the diner. Grand Falls looked even better in the sunlight. Maggie glanced about, taking it all in. It wasn't hugely busy, but there were people everywhere. The mercantile seemed more than a little busy, with a constant flow of customers.

"The mercantile is owned by Cecil Delbert and his wife Hannah," Mrs. Baker told her. "I'll introduce you later, since I may send you over there for supplies." She waved to someone in the distance as they crossed the road toward the diner.

Unlocking the door, she turned to Maggie. "I thought you could start by serving the customers. If that works for you." She returned the key to her pocket and locked the door behind them. "It's a good way to get to know the lay of the diner, as well as the locals. Once you're comfortable, we can talk about you helping in the kitchen." She raised her eyebrows as if seeking confirmation.

"Fine with me," Maggie said, but she wasn't certain she was. She had been looking forward to doing some cooking and helping her most generous hostess. On the other hand, serving customers would also be very helpful to Mrs. Baker. The woman was obviously run off her feet and could do with the help.

"Of course, before the diner opens, I could use your help with the preparations." Maggie stared at her in confusion. "Cooking, my dear girl. At least getting everything ready for the cooking. Stew is first to be made, since it takes the longest to be ready."

That sounded more like what Maggie was interested in, but whatever she could do to help would make her happy. She was a complete stranger, and yet, Mrs. Baker hadn't hesitated in offering Maggie accommodation in her own home. It was the least she could do to thank the woman.

"First, though," she said with a smile. "We put the water on to boil for coffee." Once that chore was done, she pulled out a well-worn recipe book. "Do you think you could make the muffins while I start work on the stew?"

She began strolling around the large kitchen. "Bowls are in this cupboard, you'll find pans in here, and most of the ingredients you'll need are here." She opened the recipe book and turned to the correct page. "Could you make a double batch? Blueberries are the flavor of the day. I try to change it each day."

Warmth flooded Maggie. Muffins were one of her favorite things to make. She'd learned with those and had gone on from there. Although not the best of cooks, she'd learned enough to get by. "Of course. How many are in a batch?"

"Twenty-four. My muffins are very popular." She turned away then, and busied herself with cutting the beef for the stew. The large pot was already heating on the stove, and Maggie was astonished at the size of the pot. Did Mrs. Baker intend to feed a small army?

Maggie reached into the cupboard and pulled out a large bowl, then collected up all the ingredients she needed. She measured out the flour, eggs, and milk, as well as sugar, then stirred until the mix was free of lumps. "Where are the blueberries?" she asked, glancing about the room. "I can't find them."

"Are they not in the icebox?"

Maggie checked again. "They don't appear to be."

"What a nuisance. I'll have to go to the mercantile for more," she said, cleaning her hands.

"I can go," Maggie told her. "Is there anything else you need while I'm there?"

A smile split the older woman's face. "That would be very helpful. I can't think of anything else I need. Make sure Cecil and Hannah add it to my account."

Maggie pulled the apron over her head and strolled across the road. From what Mrs. Baker told her the previous night, Grand Falls was a growing town. It had been quite static for some years, but more recently, the local carpenters, Sawdust Harry and Patrick Harper, expanded the town by building houses even before they sold. The past months had seen many new townsfolk arrive. She wasn't certain if Mrs. Baker thought that was a good thing or not.

The thought made her smile.

"Good morning."

"Good morning. You must be Hannah? I am Maggie Coulter. I'm helping Mrs. Baker at the diner for a few days."

"Welcome," Hannah said. She appeared genuinely happy to see the newcomer. "What can I do for you today?"

"The diner needs blueberries. Mrs. Baker said you carry them."

The storekeeper moved toward an area reserved for produce. "How many do you need?"

"About four cups would do nicely, thank you."

Hannah measured the blueberries and placed them in a paper bag, then added them to the diner's account. "There you are. I'm sure we'll see each other again soon."

"Oh, I'm not staying," Maggie insisted. "I'm merely passing through."

Hannah grinned and patted Maggie's hand. *Did she know something Maggie didn't?* Her plan had always been to stay only one night. That was now extended to another two, three days at most, to help her hostess. After that, Maggie would leave, traveling until she found somewhere that appealed to her. When that happened, she would settle down. She doubted she would ever return permanently to Shady Hollow, where she'd come from. Of course, she would visit her parents from time to time, but that's where it would end. The last thing she needed was to come face to face with Marcus. Hopefully, by the time she returned, he was married and settled with a family. She truly wished him all the best and hoped the woman he would eventually marry loved him back.

"Thank you again," Maggie said as she headed out the door. She smiled as the bell over the door tingled. Mrs. Baker had one similar. "I'm back," she called as she entered the diner again, then locked the door as Mrs. Baker had done earlier. She'd explained at the time customers would arrive at all hours of the day if the door wasn't locked. Apparently, the diner owner didn't like when that happened.

Entering the kitchen, she giggled at the flour-covered cook. Maggie was suddenly grateful she hadn't been around at the time. Flour filled the air and covered the kitchen counter. "What happened?" she asked, suddenly curious.

"I dropped the tin." Her new friend looked exasperated with herself. "The darn thing slipped right out of my hands. Such a nuisance, but it will be easy enough to clean up. We need to finish our preparations first as the customers won't wait for us to finish cooking."

Maggie tipped the blueberries into the large bowl with the batter and stirred gently until they were dispersed throughout the mix. She greased the tins, then distributed the mix evenly, finally adding them to the oven.

She glanced across to see the beef sizzling away in the large pot, and offered to help in whatever way she could. "If you could peel those potatoes, it would be a great help," Mrs. Baker told Maggie.

Maggie washed the bowl she'd used previously and peeled the potatoes. Once peeled and washed, she cut them into smaller pieces as instructed. Then she helped with the carrots. She'd never made stew before, so this was a lesson for her as well. Maggie wished she'd listened to her mother more often. If she had, she would likely be much more help right now.

Mrs. Baker glanced at the large clock on the wall. "Time to get the soup on – it is my best seller at lunch time. Once that is done, I'll have to prepare the biscuits." She turned to Maggie then. "Have you made biscuits before?"

"Once or twice," Maggie said gingerly. "If you have a recipe, I'm good at following directions." *Unless I'm being told to marry someone I don't love*, she pondered.

"Wonderful!" Mrs. Baker became quite animated at the revelation. How she managed by herself, Maggie had no idea. But she was pleased she was there to help when her companion needed it most.

The diner owner flicked through her tattered recipe book once more and found the biscuit recipe. "It's the plain recipe we want today. We'll make the cheese ones another day." *Except I won't be here for that*, Maggie mused. It seemed like everyone was hoping she would stay, but Grand Falls wasn't part of her long terms plans.

"Oh blast," Mrs. Baker suddenly said. "I'm not sure there's enough flour now, since I dropped the tin and wasted a good portion of it." She appeared quite annoyed with herself. Then an unfamiliar emotion came over her. *Was it panic?* Maggie honestly didn't know, since she didn't know the woman well enough.

She reached out and put a hand on Mrs. Baker's shoulder, staring down into her face. Although she was far older, she reminded Maggie of her mother. She would hate to see her mother in this situation, running a diner by herself, without the help she desperately needed. "I can take care of the soup while you finish up the stew." A grateful smile spread over the other woman's face.

"That would be most helpful," she said. "How long did you say can you could stay?"

Maggie sighed inwardly. She knew this could become an issue, but had to ensure she wasn't enticed into staying far longer than necessary. Not that she thought Marcus would come looking for her. If that were to happen, surely he would have been here by now? "I can stay a few more days if it helps," she said firmly, not wanting to give any false hope.

Mrs. Baker nodded, but was clearly disappointed. "You can't stay longer? I thought you had no specific plans."

It was true. Maggie had no specific plans, and there was no reason she couldn't stay a week or two. But that was it. After that time, she would move on. "I can probably stay another week or so. Would that help?"

"Thank you, my dear. That would be an enormous help." Maggie found herself wrapped in a big bear hug, despite the small stature of her new friend. When she looked down, she could have sworn she saw a tear leak out of the other woman's eye.

Maggie unlocked the diner door precisely at noon, as instructed.

There were already several customers waiting. Maggie held the door wide and stepped aside. She writhed under the scrutiny she received, but tried not to take it personally. She was, after all, a stranger in town. Few people had met her, so naturally there would be curiosity surrounding her existence.

The customers hurried toward their table of choice, and Maggie was grateful she'd prepared each table before the doors opened. She introduced herself to each customer, then handed them a menu, promising to return shortly. She was far more nervous than she'd expected. This was her first-ever job, even if she wasn't being paid. Her services were bartered in return for room and board, and Maggie didn't mind in the least.

She hurried to the kitchen and snatched up a pencil and the notepad used for taking orders. The lunch menu only had a few items on it. It was a service to the customers for the diner to be opened this early, she'd been told. Traditionally the diner had only opened for supper, but since her husband had died, Mrs. Baker liked to keep busy, so opened earlier.

In Maggie's opinion, that wasn't necessarily a good thing, as the elderly woman was run off her feet. She needed an assistant, another pair of hands. Maggie was enjoying helping, but wondered what would happen once she left. *Would Mrs. Baker struggle again?* She couldn't bear to think about it.

After taking each table's order, Maggie returned to the kitchen with the order, then took water to each table. She couldn't remember walking so much in one day her entire life. Nonetheless, she was enjoying herself. It was certainly different from anything she'd even done before. Plus, it was helping her new friend immensely.

She turned as the bell over the door jingled once more. Maggie had begun to dislike that bell – it seemed every time she thought things had died down, another customer arrived. As she took the orders to the kitchen, she glanced across at the latest customer entering the diner.

He looked vaguely familiar, but she couldn't fathom why. It was unlikely she'd run into him anywhere else. Apart from eating right here in the diner, she'd been to the livery to accommodate her horse yesterday, and the mercantile today.

The newcomer found an empty table at the back of the room, and glanced about, then slid down his chair. He appeared rather deflated, so Maggie hurried over and handed him a menu. "Welcome," she said cheerfully, and he glanced up briefly, but seemed far from happy.

"You're new," he said, then turned to the menu.

"I'm Maggie," she said cheerfully, but he didn't introduce himself or even acknowledge her, except for an almost inaudible grunt. He was clearly unhappy, so Maggie left him to himself until he was in a better frame of mind.

Instead, she hurried into the kitchen and collected the other orders that were ready for distribution. Snatching up a tray, she grabbed the orders. As she was about to leave, she commented on the latest customer. "You have a very unhappy customer out there." She started out of the room.

"Where?" Mrs. Baker asked, craning her neck to see.

"Up the back, in the corner. I couldn't even get him to introduce himself." The older woman hurried out of the kitchen, Maggie's eyes following her every move as she delivered the meals.

"Tucker," she heard her new boss say. "I was sorry to hear about your father. How is your mother doing? And Charlie?"

His head shot up. "Better than they've been in years now that miserable old fool is dead." He rubbed a hand across his face. "I should never have left them alone. It's a wonder he didn't kill them both."

It was all Maggie could do not to gasp.

"Charlie learned to fight back," Mrs. Baker said quietly. "You had your own life to live."

He stared into the old lady's face as she slid down and sat next to him. "That's what Ma said, but it still cuts me to the core. At least she kicked him out once Charlie proved himself stronger."

Maggie watched the interaction between the two. Obviously, this man's father had died, but it was more than a little apparent there was no love lost between the two.

"What will you do now?"

Tucker glanced at the menu, apparently trying to avoid looking at Mrs. Baker. "I'll probably sell the livery." He glanced up then. "Or I could keep it and let Charlie run it. He's done a good job until now. From what I've heard, that vile old drunk hasn't been near the place for some time. All the better for my brother."

Mrs. Baker nodded, but didn't respond – she just let the man speak, which, from what Maggie could see, was probably what he needed. She could not hear any more of the conversation as she left then, to clear the tables, and then returned to the kitchen.

She rinsed the dishes, and as she walked out the kitchen door, almost knocked Mrs. Baker over. The woman looked distressed. "Are you all right?" she asked softly. The moment she did, Maggie wished she'd kept quiet. Perhaps Mrs. Baker didn't want to discuss it.

"That's Tucker Smith, from the livery," she whispered. "His mongrel father recently died, so he's returned to town."

"For the funeral?"

Mrs. Baker laughed. "No one attended his funeral," she said. "He returned to help sort out the business." She then hurried on to finish preparing the meals that were waiting to be plated. Maggie sensed there was far more to the story, but it wasn't her business. Besides, she'd be gone soon.

"Can you take this coffee over to Tucker, please? I have a feeling he needs it more than the food." Maggie took the mug and carried it to the customer without another word.

She placed it on the table in front of him, and he glanced up. "Thanks," he mumbled, then took a sip. "I'm Tucker," he almost whispered. "Sorry about before."

"Don't even think about it," Maggie said, smiling.

He glanced up at her, and despite his disheveled look and his unshaven face, he smiled, and Maggie almost melted.

Chapter Three

"I'll clean up – you take a break. You look completely done in," Maggie told her friend.

Mrs. Baker waved her concerns aside. "I'm fine. More hands make light work, as they say." She poured them both a mug of coffee and placed them on a table near the kitchen. "But first, we eat." Then she returned to the kitchen, and after dishing up thick vegetable soup for each of them, carried the bowls to the table. Maggie followed with the leftover biscuits.

The blessing was said, then Mrs. Baker looked her square in the face. "You look exhausted. Tonight will be even busier; the supper service always is." She began to eat. "I'm not sure you should stay for that."

Maggie's hackles rose. "I'm far younger than you. If you can do it, then so can I." Her companion grinned.

"We'll see." She then concentrated on the food in front of her. "After we've eaten and cleaned up from lunch, we will take a break, then prepare for this evening. I'll need to check the supplies, in case we need to get anything from the mercantile."

Maggie nodded. That seemed reasonable.

"The stew is progressing nicely, and I have a roast ready to put in the oven. We'll make another batch of soup – that's always quite popular," she said. "Sometimes we even run out."

Maggie listened carefully. These were things she needed to know. No doubt they would prepare lots of vegetable for the roast, not to mention the soup. For a seemingly quiet town, the diner was rather busy.

"I usually go home for a couple of hours between lunch and supper. Otherwise, it's not really a break, is it?" The old lady smiled, and it warmed Maggie's heart.

Stopping here was meant to be for one night only. Once she'd stayed the extra days as promised, she would move on to the next town until she found somewhere to forget her troubles. To forget she'd run from her own wedding, effectively ruining her life, and that of her betrothed.

Why oh why didn't she put her foot down far earlier? Tell Marcus she didn't want to marry him? But Maggie knew the answer to that question – everyone else decided for her. Since she'd been schooled to do whatever she was told to do, she complied. Rebelling was not in her blood. How she wished it was.

The pair finished lunch, then cleaned up. They checked the food that was already cooking, added the roast to the oven, then left for home.

Home.

Mrs. Baker's house felt more like home than her parent's home had for quite some time. The last months had been filled with wedding arrangements. Marcus wanted to make the day special for her. Memorable.

It was certainly that, but for all the wrong reasons.

Maggie didn't know what came over her. As she walked down that aisle, she knew she couldn't go through with the marriage, despite knowing she would have a good life, a peaceful life. Marcus had a housekeeper. The woman did all the cooking, the laundry, cleaning. Everything.

That didn't mean she would have a happy life.

What was left for Maggie to do, apart from bearing his children? Besides, she didn't love Marcus. When she'd told him, he seemed a little hurt, but insisted she would come to love him.

Hadn't she already had enough time? They'd known each other for years. Not weeks or months. Years.

She shook herself mentally. Maggie was torturing herself, and for what? She had done the right thing.

She knew she had. Truth be told, given time, Marcus would believe the same thing. Perhaps that was why he didn't come after her. He knew the truth already, because she'd told him. Her running away almost certainly confirmed it.

"Why don't you lay down for a while, my dear?" The words were music to her ears, but Maggie didn't want to let her new friend down.

"I'm sure there's something I can do to help?"

Mrs. Baker smiled. "I'm going to lie down myself. I'm plumb worn out." Maggie didn't doubt it for a moment. *How old must the woman be? At least seventy?* She should have retired by now, sold the diner, and be living a peaceful life. But Maggie could see as much as it wore her down, she enjoyed it. Not the hard work associated with it, but talking to people, socializing. The woman reveled in it, and that was plain for everyone to see, including those who barely knew her.

She went into her bedroom and kicked off her shoes. Every muscle in her body ached, and she could barely keep her eyes open. As she drifted off to sleep, Maggie realized she'd enjoyed every moment of her time today.

Especially meeting one particular customer who wore his regret on his face.

The food preparation for this evening was done, and the desserts were made and ready to place in the oven. Maggie stretched. Her back ached from all the standing. "If you can spare me, I'd like to visit Daisy and make sure she's all right."

"Daisy?"

"My horse. She was a gift from Marcus, so at least I don't have horse stealing hanging over my head."

Mrs. Baker nodded. "Is he a vindictive man, this Marcus?" She studied Maggie carefully, and she almost writhed under the other woman's gaze.

"Not to my knowledge, but you never know what might trigger that sort of response, I suppose." Maggie removed her apron and ran her hands down her skirt. "Am I presentable?"

"You're perfectly fine since you're visiting a horse and not a suitor." Mrs. Baker chuckled, and Maggie ran her hands over her face and hair. "I was joking, my dear. You are acceptable. No flour on your face, and not a hair out of place. Off you go then. Take your time."

Maggie put on her bonnet as she headed to the front door. She glanced about. There were a few people on the street. The town was far larger than Shady Hollow, but was nowhere near as busy. That was the beauty of a newish town, she supposed. One that was growing, but not yet over-populated.

As she made her way toward the livery, Maggie took in the buildings. There was a wonderful variety of stores. It meant she would never need to travel to another town to shop.

She paused. *Where did that come from?* Maggie had no intention of staying in Grand Falls and had already decided to move on after she'd fulfilled her promise to Mrs. Baker. She was only here now to help her new friend, the elderly lady who needed a break.

She shook herself mentally and continued on her way. As she entered the livery, she spotted the young man who had helped her when she'd arrived. He was tending to Daisy, feeding her oats. Daisy's head went up when she spotted Maggie, and her heart filled with joy.

"Hullo Miss," Charlie called. "She's been pining for you."

"I've missed her too," Maggie almost whispered. When she moved closer, Daisy nudged her. "Thank you for looking after her. It looks like I'll be here for another day or two. Will that be an inconvenience?" She already had the coins in her hands, ready to pay the required fee.

"Not an inconvenience at all." Charlie's head spun around to face his brother, Tucker. He scowled, but said not a word. From the little Mrs. Baker had told Maggie, Tucker was now the legal owner of the livery. That likely irked Charlie no end, since he'd been running the establishment for quite some time. "Good day to you, Miss Maggie," Tucker said as he tipped his hat. "Your horse is safe with us. As you can see," he glanced about, his hand pointing toward several empty stalls, "we're not exactly overflowing."

"Thank you, Tucker. I appreciate it." She reached out to give him the coins she had in her hand. Instead of taking the money, Tucker's hand wrapped around her own. A shiver went down her spine, and she glanced up into his face. He didn't speak, but his expression told Maggie he felt it too. They stood staring at each other for several heartbeats – hers was so loud, Maggie couldn't gauge how long it had been. It might only have been a matter of seconds, but it felt like a lifetime.

She continued to stare into his face, until she finally pulled her hand away, realizing the coins were still there. The last thing she wanted was to repeat the experience she'd just had, although she certainly wasn't complaining. Tucker seemed to have some sort of pull on her. She felt enamored by him – something she'd never felt with Marcus.

Tucker reached out, apparently coming to the same conclusion Maggie had, but instead of risking touching him again, she let the coins slip from her fingers. He glanced at her, and then at the coins.

And then he laughed. Finally, he leaned down and took the coins from the dirt.

After wiping the coins on his pants, he glanced at the money he held. "This is too much," he said, endeavoring to hand some of it back.

She studied him for mere moments. "Keep it. I'll likely be here longer. Mrs. Baker needs the help."

"If you're certain? Follow me to the office and I'll add this to your account." He didn't wait for a response, but turned, leaving Maggie no choice but to follow.

The office was tiny. With Tucker inside, there was barely room left for another person. He was tall; she didn't even reach his shoulder, and the man was solid, all muscle. Now that he'd cleaned up, she could see he was quite handsome. Her first impression of him was not the best, but today he seemed far better. Happier even. Perhaps whatever Mrs. Baker said to him last night at the diner had helped. She hoped so, because he was beyond miserable when he'd first arrived.

He opened the account book and turned the pages, looking for her account. It appeared to be a fruitless exercise. "Did Charlie set up an account for you?"

She frowned. The last thing she wanted was to get Charlie in trouble. "I doubt it. My plan was to stay one night, then leave this morning." She shrugged.

"Mrs. Baker asked me to stay a little longer, so here I am."

"I see," he said bitterly, as he wrote her name at the top of a clean page. He added the previous night's lodgings for Daisy, then added the amount she'd given him just minutes ago.

His manner changed so quickly, Maggie couldn't fathom the problem. Then it hit her – Charlie was pocketing the proceeds for a single night stay. Tucker had realized it the moment he couldn't find her details in the account book.

Maggie felt terrible. She didn't want Charlie to get into trouble on her behalf, but knew deep down it wasn't her fault or her problem. "Don't you worry about it," Tucker said gently. "Charlie boy learned to look out for himself and ma when our pa was alive. Bad habits are hard to break, I guess." He grimaced then, and she knew he was again admonishing himself for leaving them to their own defenses against their pa. "Would you like to take Miss Daisy for a ride?" He seemed far more cheerful than before. "I could come with you." He brushed his overgrown hair off his face as he stood. "If you want to, that is. I'd hate for you to get lost."

Her heart fluttered. She wanted nothing more than to ride Daisy – it had been a while. But she didn't have a saddle, nor did she have her riding clothes.

"I…" she glanced up into his face. "I don't have a saddle. I came in that buggy over there."

"If that's all that's holding you back, I can lend you a saddle." He looked her up and down. "But I don't have women's riding clothes." He laughed then, and Maggie's heart fluttered again. She knew she shouldn't, but she was quickly warming to Tucker. A man who was as troubled as she was. Perhaps even more so.

"I'm willing to take the risk if you are," she whispered. Tucker headed toward the tack room and pulled down a well-worn saddle. It wasn't long before they were heading out of town.

Tucker felt a tinge of guilt at leaving Charlie to run the livery alone. He soon realized, though, his younger brother had been doing so for sometime now, and getting little in return. It was the reason Charlie had been pocketing much of the proceeds.

Charlie might have been running the business alone, but his father owned it, and kept all the profits for himself. He had reluctantly paid Charlie a meagre *wage*. It seemed to Tucker it was their father's way of punishing Charlie for standing up to their violent father.

Now that Tucker was the legal owner of the livery, things would change, already had changed. Charlie now received a decent wage – one that would allow him to live comfortably, and not on the verge of poverty.

"It's beautiful here," Maggie said as she glanced about. "Thank you for bringing me here." She smiled and his heart fluttered. The pair barely knew each other. *How could she make him feel this way?*

He took a restorative breath, allowing himself to calm down. This was not a date, he was merely showing a new friend the area. "If we had the time, I'd take you further up the mountain. Maybe have a picnic by the stream."

Maggie glanced down into her lap, her expression solemn. "I'm only staying another day or two. I promised to help Edna Baker, to give her a break. She's worked herself into the ground."

Tucker nodded sadly, but wasn't sure why her statement cut through his heart. They only just met, and were mere acquaintances; he couldn't even say they were friends. "I thought you might stay a little longer," he almost whispered.

"Honestly," she said, staring off into the distance. "I have no specific plans. I'm still trying to work it all out."

Her comment was cryptic. Tucker had absolutely no idea why Maggie was in Grand Falls, but if she wanted him to know, she would tell him. That much he knew. Instead of answering, he nodded, then gave a little grunt. He immediately felt embarrassed at such a sound, especially doing it to a lady like Maggie. "I'm a bit like that myself," he admitted. "I only came home for my brother and ma.

He would have never left Grand Falls, but ma insisted. After the beating pa had given Tucker's mother, he'd beat the heck out of the monster. By that time, Charlie was big enough to fight back as well, and they ganged up on him. Got him out of the house and made sure ma was safe from him. When ma saw an advertisement for a job on a ranch in another town, she insisted he apply. Said he needed to live his life and earn his own money.

None of that appeased his guilt. Now that Bart Smith was dead, they could all breathe easy. He would help Charlie built the livery back up to its past glory and then decide his future. Right now, everything was a jumble in his mind. Tucker hadn't decided whether to stay in Grand Falls permanently, or whether he would go back to his job. His boss had given him time off to get his thoughts together, and Tucker appreciated that more than he could put into words.

Maggie glanced up at him momentarily. "Mrs. Baker told me about your situation. I hope you don't mind."

He nodded again, and almost grunted, but pulled himself up in time. He ran a hand across his chin. He must look a mess. At least he had to look better than yesterday. *Did he mind?* Tucker wasn't certain, but the cat was out of the bag, and it was too late to put it back. "The whole town knows, so why not you too," he said, trying not to sound bitter. "My father was a gigantic failure, and a violent man. His drinking ruined my family's lives. Now that he's gone, life will be better." He glanced up at her, certain he must appear self-serving. "Far better."

"I'm so terribly sorry."

"Not about my father, I hope." He raised his eyebrows, but was almost certain she wasn't giving him sympathy where it wasn't wanted. Or needed.

She stared at him momentarily, then pulled her eyes away. "Absolutely not. I'm sorry for what you and your family endured." She reached out and clasped his hand. Warmth flooded him, and Tucker wasn't sure what to make of it. They'd only met the night before at the diner, and here he was feeling things he had no right to feel. He shook himself mentally.

He was sorely tempted to cover her hand with his own, but resisted the urge. At her own admission, Maggie wasn't staying in town. She did not know how long she was staying, and neither did he. As much as he felt a connection to her, things were up in the air for them both.

He glanced up at the sky. "We'd better head back if you intend to help Mrs. Baker with the evening service." She seemed disappointed, which matched exactly how Tucker was feeling. Somehow, Maggie made him feel better about himself. She exuded a calmness he hadn't felt before.

Or was it simply because his father was no longer a threat to his family?

Chapter Four

Maggie arrived back at the diner in plenty of time to help Mrs. Baker, but felt guilty at not being there for much of the afternoon.

"Did you enjoy your ride?" She had a smile on her wrinkled face.

Maggie's head spun around. "How…how did you know?"

The older woman chuckled. "I went outside for a breath of fresh air and saw the pair of you leaving on the horses. So…was it good? What do you think of Tucker?"

Was the woman trying to match them? Surely not. In the past several days, Maggie had fled her wedding, wandered aimlessly, and finally arrived in Grand Falls. She was far from seeking a husband. Especially after her last experience. The last thing she needed or wanted was to be matched up again. If only her family and Marcus' family had left them alone, things might have been different.

She shook her head. Maggie knew that wasn't true. They had been friends, good friends, but they were not in love. At least she wasn't. Marcus had professed his love for her, and she had believed him, but now realized it was far from the truth. She was eligible, from a good family, and they liked each other. That was not love, and it wasn't the best way to start a marriage, either.

She did not regret running away. Not one iota. If she hadn't, she would be married now. She would also be living the high life in Helena on their honeymoon. Maggie *still* didn't regret her actions. She was more of a small town homebody type. She believed it to be the reason Marcus had chosen her. Many of the other spinsters in Shady Hollow liked to attend parties, to dine at the best restaurants, and spend their money on clothes and shoes.

Maggie was the exact opposite. She adored home cooking, preferred to stay home, and when it came to clothes, her mother had to almost drag her to the store to update her wardrobe.

The bell over the door jingled, and Maggie couldn't believe it. Surely it wasn't that late? The diner opened at five, and she thought she'd returned in plenty of time. She turned to her *boss,* feeling quite dismayed. "I'm so sorry. I did not know it was this late."

Mrs. Baker scrutinized her. "I've managed on my own for many years. Don't you worry yourself. I'm glad you enjoyed your afternoon with young Tucker. You both deserve a bit of happiness."

Young Tucker?, she almost blurted out. Then realized he was young compared to the older woman. "He told me what happened," Maggie said, still feeling sadness over his situation.

"Good. I'm glad he did." She clapped her hands together. "Customers are arriving. We need to get to it."

Maggie headed to the door and escorted the first group of customers to their table. When she turned around, a group of three stood waiting to be seated. It was Tucker, his brother, and a woman she presumed to be their mother. The sadness hit her all over again. The three seemed to be encased by a halo of gloom, although she now knew it was not the death of the father made them sad, but for the life they had endured until he was gone.

She put on her best smile and headed their way. "Hello Tucker, Charlie," she said. "Glad to meet you, Mrs. Smith. I can give you the best table in the diner," she said with a wink, and Tucker grinned.

"There's no need to do that." Mrs. Smith seemed adamant.

"The place is almost empty, Ma." Tucker reassured his mother, and reached for Maggie's hand. She felt the heat creep up her face, and turned away, leading them to the table she'd promised. It was away from the kitchen, and also the front door. It was a quiet spot up the back of the room, and truly was the best table in the diner. "We appreciate it," Tucker said, keeping close to her as he followed.

Once seated, Maggie handed each of them a menu. "Roast lamb is the special tonight. I'll be back shortly with water." She scurried away before her heart could flutter any longer. Being near Tucker sent her nerve endings askew, and Maggie didn't know why. For someone she'd only just met, strange things were happening. Things she'd never encountered before. Not with Marcus, nor anyone else.

It left her feeling quite confused. Then she realized – she felt sorry for Tucker, and his family too. Life had dealt them a terrible blow with Bart Smith. From what she'd been told, everyone in town knew the situation, and as much as they tried to protect the family, it wasn't always possible. It was the reason the business had gone downhill. No one wanted to support the man. Unfortunately, it only made matters worse for the family.

Maggie carried a jug of water and three glasses back to the table, then poured water into each glass. She hovered for a moment, trying to gauge if they were ready to order. Tucker glanced up and smiled. Her heart pounded. She tried to ignore her reaction and held her pencil over the order pad. "Are you ready to order?" she asked in a shaky voice. *What was wrong with her?*

"Roast lamb for three," Tucker said, then added, "Plus coffee for two, and tea for one. Thanks Maggie."

"Will you be having dessert?" She hated asking this early in the evening, but it was how the diner had always worked.

"Can we decide after we've eaten the main course?" Mrs. Smith asked with a tentative smile.

"Of course." Maggie placed a napkin on each person's lap and startled when Tucker gently touched her hand. She glanced down at him and grinned, then pulled her hand away. "I have to go," she whispered and headed off.

"That Tucker is something else, isn't he?" Mrs. Baker chuckled.

Had she been watching? Maggie was sure she had. The woman could be cunning, there was no doubt, but apparently her mind had been made up. Maggie had to ensure she resisted all moves to get her and Tucker together. Especially since neither of them was interested in anything but friendship.

With the dinner service over, and the kitchen finally cleaned up, the ladies headed out of the diner. They found Tucker waiting outside. "Tucker," Mrs. Baker said dryly. "What are you doing here?" No doubt the other woman already had an inkling.

Maggie was beginning to understand how she thought.

Tucker said momentarily, then grinned. "I decided to accompany you lovely ladies home."

"More like Maggie," she said under her breath, but her voice was quite audible. She turned to him and smiled then. "Go on, then. Off you go." She motioned for them to go ahead.

"That is never going to happen," Tucker said firmly. "I couldn't live with myself if something were to happen to you." He hooked Maggie's arm through his and moved off, ensuring all three stayed together.

The old lady pouted. "How do you think I get home every night? I don't have someone to escort me there. Never have since my dear Henry passed on." She lifted her chin, as though proving a point. "I've not once had a problem." She looked him up and down then. "You've never offered before either, young fella." She chuckled then and hurried ahead of them.

Maggie couldn't help but laugh, and Tucker joined her. "She has a point," he mumbled. "Supper was good," he suddenly said through the silence of the evening.

Knowing he was just making small talk to fill the awkward gap when no one spoke, she agreed, but then all was quiet again. It wasn't far from the little cottage Mrs. Baker and her husband bought many years earlier, even before they had purchased the diner. The older woman told her earlier that evening, they'd never been blessed with children, and so the diner had become their lives. Until Henry had died suddenly.

Maggie felt sorry for her hostess. She was a nice person. From what she'd already seen for herself, Mrs. Baker was kind to everyone. She enjoyed the company of others, and also enjoyed cooking. The diner was perfect for her, except it was now far too much work for her to do alone.

It got Maggie to thinking – could she take over the diner? Temporarily at least, and give the owner a break? Not an hour or two as she had done earlier today, but days or even weeks? She shook her head. Her boss would never go for it, even if she did need time off.

She would think about it a little longer and try to come up with a plan that would be acceptable. In the meantime, she would enjoy the company of Tucker Smith, whose presence filled her with joy. She glanced at him and Tucker smiled. Maggie liked him, but she'd only known him a couple of days. Besides, she wasn't interested in anything more than friendship.

She would stay long enough to help Mrs. Baker out – after all, she'd taken Maggie in when she needed it most – and then she would be gone. She'd leave Grand Falls forever, and continue to wander about the countryside until she found the place she belonged.

Until then, she'd make the most of her time here. If that meant spending time with Tucker Smith, then so be it.

Tucker glanced across at her. "Are you all right? You seem deep in thought."

She nodded. "I'm fine. I was thinking about my future." He stared deep into her eyes, his expression somber. "I'm not sure where I'll be this time next week. I guess I should start planning."

He continued to stare at her. Maggie couldn't fathom what he was thinking. "You're leaving?" he finally asked, sounding quite deflated.

"I…" She was more than a little flabbergasted. *Did he want her to stay?* "Honestly, I don't know what I'm doing. I arrived here by chance."

His expression now questioning, she wasn't sure whether she should tell him her story or not.

"We're here." Mrs. Baker's voice rumbled through the night, startling Maggie with its loudness. "Goodnight Tucker," she said forcefully, and there was no doubt she had no intention of inviting their escort in.

"Goodnight," he said. "I'll probably see you tomorrow."

"If you must," Mrs. Baker said, but Maggie was certain she was simply niggling at Tucker, seeing if he would retaliate. He never did, but instead, turned and walked away.

"Goodnight," she whispered, and then he was gone. Maggie didn't know why she felt disappointed he gave in so easily.

Maggie rushed toward the church as she heard the bell ringing. "Oh my gosh, we're late," she said, grabbing her reticule as they left the cottage.

"I doubt it," Mrs. Baker replied. "They ring that darned bell for around twenty minutes every Sunday morning. I'm sure they do it to ensure everyone is out of bed in time for the service."

Maggie smiled at the thought. *Was it the preacher's way of getting more people to attend services?* If so, it would surely be unique. Not that she would be impressed if she lived close by and was awakened by the bell. That wouldn't be fun at all.

As they made their way along the main street, Maggie was surprised by the number of people also heading that way. They had good attendance at Shady Hollow, but it was sporadic because of the large number of outlying ranches. Regulars consisted mainly of those who lived in town. Marcus was one of the few ranch owners who attended regularly. It was something she'd loved about him until she came to realize it was his way of trying to win her over.

What a fool she'd been. It made her wonder if she'd also been fooled by his wealth. Her parents had convinced her marrying Marcus was the right thing to do. For them, perhaps, as it heightened their standing in the community. But for Maggie, it would have been a disaster. *Why didn't anyone worry about how it would affect her?*

In her rush to get there, she tripped on the boardwalk, but firm hands stopped her from falling. She gasped, but Maggie wasn't sure if it was because she almost fell, or because she'd been saved. When she glanced up, warmth flooded her at seeing Tucker standing in front of her. The first thing she noticed was his chocolate brown eyes.

Why hadn't she noticed them before? Perhaps because she'd avoided looking at them previously. The last thing Maggie wanted was to become close to any man. Even as a friend. She would be gone from Grand Falls within the week, and the last thing she needed was a broken heart.

She almost sputtered at the thought. *Why would she have a broken heart?* She wasn't in love with Tucker – she barely knew the man. He did, however, cause her heart to flutter over the strangest things. Simply standing close to him sent shivers down her spine, and when he touched her, warmth flooded her.

The best thing Maggie could do was to keep her distance. *Right at this moment, though?* He was standing so close she could feel his breath on her cheek. "Are you all right? Anything hurt?"

With Maggie standing at the top of the steps, and Tucker at the bottom, they were face to face. She felt mesmerized, and was frozen to the spot. She ran her hands down her skirts and twisted her ankle around. "I'm fine. Nothing broken, twisted, or cut." She tried to smile, but she was certain it came out as a grimace. Without another word, Tucker reached out and took her hand, helping Maggie down the steps.

She heard Mrs. Baker chuckle behind her. For someone who appeared to be discouraging Tucker, she seemed pretty happy.

"Charlie and ma have gone on ahead. I thought it would be nice for us to walk to church together." When she looked at him, Tucker looked happy. The sadness that had overtaken him seemed to have dissipated. It made him look even more handsome than before. Of course, the suit he wore probably made a difference as well.

When Tucker slipped his arm through hers, Maggie felt a flutter run down her spine. She had none of these feelings with Marcus. The romance novels she read mentioned all these things. When she'd mentioned it to her mother, Maggie was told to throw the books in the trash – they were fiction and far from the truth.

Maggie complied, but now it had her wondering.

Charlie and Mrs. Smith had saved places for the three of them. The moment Maggie stepped inside that church, peace overcame her. She'd been conflicted about dumping her marriage to Marcus, right up until the point she'd ran. Once she'd done so, she knew she'd done the right thing, but then guilt overtook her. The one thing she understood for certain was her parents would be incredibly upset with her. They would be ridiculed by the people of Shady Hollow, not Maggie, simply by the fact she wasn't there.

If she could do it over again, Maggie would still run. This time, though, she wouldn't let it get as far as the actual wedding day. Nor would she walk down the aisle. She would stand firm, and wouldn't allow herself to be manipulated by her family or by

Marcus. She was an adult and needed to make her own decisions.

One of her favorite hymns was playing, and Maggie reveled in the sound. She sat down next to Tucker, and Mrs. Baker sat by Mrs. Smith. The two women exchanged a few words before the room went silent. The preacher – Preacher Angus Devon, Tucker had told her – greeted the congregation, and said a brief prayer. He then welcomed Maggie into the fold. *Did he not know she wasn't staying in Grand Falls?* Still, it was a friendly gesture and she would be sure to thank him.

The sermon talked about helping your neighbor. From what she had seen so far, this was a town where everyone helped everyone else. Just as Maggie intended to help Mrs. Baker. The question was, would the older woman accept Maggie's offer in the vein it was meant – to give her a break?

Maggie's head was spinning. The church hall was packed.

She sipped at the coffee Tucker had made for her, and nibbled daintily at the cookie he handed her. As much as she enjoyed meeting new people, this was too much, and she was feeling overwhelmed. Almost as though he could read her mind, Tucker moved closer and slid his arm around her waist. He turned to her and winked. *Was he trying to reassure her?* Maggie thought so.

"I'd like you to meet Doctor Spencer," Tucker said. "And Mrs. Brown, Mrs. Thompson, and this is Abner Ackerman from the post office."

She smiled, then turned to Tucker. "You know I'm never going to remember everyone's name?" She turned back to her new acquaintances. "I'm pleased to meet you all."

Mrs. Brown looked her square in the face. "Are you two engaged? When is the wedding?" Maggie almost choked on her coffee. Tucker grinned.

"We're…not engaged," she sputtered. "We are just friends." She turned to Tucker, who hadn't said a word, the polecat. "We only met a few days ago when I arrived in Grand Falls."

"Uh huh," Mrs. Brown said, looking them both up and down, her eyes focusing on Tucker's arm that stayed around her waist.

Her head spun when she heard Tucker laughing. "It isn't funny!" She wanted to storm off and leave him standing there to explain himself, but that wouldn't be lady-like. Instead, she glared at him and pouted. Still not lady-like, but not so rude, and it made her feel better.

"I'm sorry," he said, still laughing. "It seems funny, you have to admit." By this time, Mrs. Brown had pinned them both down with her eyes. Maggie decided this woman was the town busy-body, and wouldn't let up until she had a reasonable explanation. She watched as Tucker pulled himself together, then turned to Mrs. Brown. "We are not engaged. As Maggie said, we only met a few days when she arrived in town. Mrs. Baker has taken her in, and Maggie is helping at the diner. That's where we met."

"Oh. You're a blow-in."

What exactly that meant, Maggie didn't know, but it didn't sound good. "If you mean am I passing through, the answer is yes. Mrs. Baker needs assistance, and I'm providing it. She is kindly housing me at her cottage."

"I see," the woman said, gazing at Maggie. *Did she not believe the truth?* More than ever, she was convinced this woman was the town gossip. What she would spread about town, Maggie dreaded to think.

"I doubt you'll see me at church next week," she said firmly. "My horse and buggy are housed at the livery, where Charlie is taking good care of them, and they'll be ready when I move on."

"Of course," Mrs. Brown said, then moved toward her next victim.

Maggie chuckled. She would forever see Mrs. Brown as the town gossip. But then she remembered today's sermon about helping your neighbor. Did that mean she couldn't hold a grudge against her? She would likely see her in the diner sometime. Secretly, she hoped not to see Mrs. Brown again. She told herself she'd have left Grand Falls before that happened.

Tucker glanced at her and shrugged. "She can be incorrigible sometimes, but she's a good old bird. She'd do anything for anyone."

"Making that assumption…" Maggie shook her head. "It's just wrong."

"What's wrong?" Mrs. Baker asked, heading toward the pair. "I hear you two are engaged. Congratulations." Her face beamed, and all Maggie's fears came to the surface.

"That's exactly what I was afraid of," Maggie said, absolutely distraught. "She's the town gossip, isn't she?" Maggie whispered. She suddenly slapped her mouth closed. She was at church, for goodness' sakes, and making accusations against a fellow parishioner. Tears welled in her eyes. She was feeling suddenly overwhelmed.

Tucker guided her outside, where the air was fresh. Mrs. Baker tagged along. After only a few days, he understood her far better than Marcus had after many years.

"Take no notice of that old biddy," Mrs. Baker said. "She lives for gossip. All she wants is to be the center of attention." She waved a hand in the air. "So, when is the wedding?" she asked, then laughed.

"It's not funny," Maggie said, then wiped a stray tear from her eye. She'd run from one wedding. *Would she be forced into another?* Not that it would be any sort of hardship to marry Tucker. She felt an affinity for him already.

Tucker stared at her. She hadn't told him why she was in Grand Falls. *Was it time?* She glanced up at Mrs. Baker, who hovered above her. Tucker sat down beside her. "What am I missing?"

"I'll leave you two lovebirds alone." With that, Mrs. Baker turned and went back inside.

"Maggie?"

She had to tell him. She knew she did. Tucker had become more than a friend, and they both knew it. She licked her lips, then turned to face him. "Last Saturday," she said quietly, "Was my wedding day."

Tucker suddenly stood. He looked stricken. "You're married?" He began to storm away.

"No, I'm not!" she shouted after him. "Please, come back and I'll tell you the whole sordid story." Tears streamed down her face, and she rummaged in her reticule for a handkerchief. Tucker stood above her and handed her his. His expression had softened, but he still looked annoyed.

Her heart was breaking. Not for herself but for Tucker – it was clear he pined for her, and she felt the same for him. She should have told him far earlier, but was afraid of his reaction. The exact reaction she had produced by not telling him.

"I…couldn't go through with it, and I ran. I got all the way down the aisle, but it didn't feel right." She glanced up at him, tears still falling. "I was forced into the marriage by my parents and his. Marcus insisted I loved him, but I didn't."

He finally sat beside her and took her hand. "I'm sorry. I shouldn't have assumed."

No, you shouldn't have, she wanted to say, but this was not Tucker's fault. The fault lay wholly with her. Besides, Tucker had his own problems to worry about. He didn't need hers to add to the stress he was under.

His arm came up around her shoulders, and he pulled her close. "I'm falling in love with you, Maggie. I don't know what I'll do if you leave." She rested her head against his chest. His heart was racing, much like her own.

Was it love she was feeling for Tucker? She really did not know. One thing she knew for certain, she'd never loved Marcus, but these feelings she had when Tucker was around – were they love? Or was it infatuation?

"I…"

He put his fingers to her lips. "Don't say anything. It's unnecessary. I want to ask you a favor." He stared lovingly into her eyes. "Would you consider staying a little longer? Give me the chance to court you?"

That was the last thing Maggie expected to hear. "Court…me?" She licked her lips – her mouth had suddenly gone dry. She still held the mug of now-cold coffee, but took a sip, her hands shaking. "No one has ever asked to court me before," she said, as she glanced down into the almost empty mug.

"Not even Marcus?"

She shook her head. He never had. He simply assumed, as he had assumed everything else. "All right. You can court me." Her tears threatened to fall again, but this time it was for happiness.

Tucker beamed. She couldn't believe how happy he seemed. It was genuine happiness too. Unlike Marcus, who seemed to feign his emotions around her. Unlike Tucker, she did not know who the real Marcus was.

"Let's go on a picnic. Our first outing with me courting you." He grinned again, and warmth flooded her.

"Oh, I can't. Mrs. Baker has a roast cooking for our lunch. But you could join us. I'm sure she wouldn't mind."

"Of course not." Her voice drifted from the doorway. "Sorted it all out, have we? Good. About time too." She chuckled, then went back inside.

Maggie had a sneaky suspicion this was the old woman's plan all along.

Chapter Five

"More potatoes, Tucker?" Mrs. Baker had been very accommodating toward Tucker, which he found a little strange. When he first met Maggie, Mrs. Baker had been a little chilly when it came to her boarder. But he knew all about the old lady's games, as well as her matchmaking antics, so nothing surprised him.

What did surprise Tucker was the fact he'd fallen for it. Or rather, he'd fallen for Maggie. Never had he imagine he would end up having feelings for a complete stranger. He needed to assess his feelings, to ensure this wasn't because of the mixed emotions he'd had since his dreadful father had died. Finally, his family was free. At least physically, they were. Mentally, he still held regrets over leaving them to Bart Smith without him. His feelings of guilt were far more than skin deep.

And now he had feelings for the young woman sitting opposite him. When he'd held her in his arms this morning, he thought his heart would explode. He'd never felt that way before. He'd held women before, so it wasn't that. But none of them made him feel the way Maggie did. One thing he knew for certain – he would have to take it slowly. She had been through a lot, and the last thing Tucker wanted was to hurt her more.

He was genuine in his feelings for her, but he did not know how she felt about him. The thing he was sure about was taking things slowly. If he went too fast, he'd scare her off, and she was sure to run again. He needed to convince her to stay, even with the premise of it being short term. *How could he do that?*

He knew she wanted to help Mrs. Baker, and he did, too. The dear woman had been incredibly kind to both Tucker and his family over the years. She'd counseled him when he returned home after his father's death. He wasn't convinced he would have coped without her kind and sensible words. She was like a grandmother to him. She had always been that way. His biggest regret was not pushing Charlie to accept her support once Tucker had left.

But things were different now. He would get the livery back to its original glory days, then hand it over to Charlie. After all, it was not something Tucker was particularly interested in. Then again, neither was working on a ranch, although he enjoyed his time there, but couldn't see himself doing that for the rest of his life.

What he would do, he did not know. It was something he would need to ponder.

"Tucker?" Mrs. Baker's voice broke through his thoughts, and Tucker startled.

"Sorry, I was thinking." He threw her a tentative smile, but the old lady frowned. "I'm all right," he said firmly. "No need to worry about me." She dished out more potatoes to his plate without another word.

It was then the idea hit him. He would need to think it over, and work out the details, but he was certain it would be beneficial not only for Mrs. Baker but also for Maggie and himself.

"The meal was delicious. Thank you." And it was delicious. His mother was an excellent cook, but Mrs. Baker was far better. Tucker patted his belly. It was full to overflowing. "Perhaps a stroll to walk off some of that delicious food?" He was looking at Maggie, but worried Mrs. Baker would take it as an invitation as well.

"Before you leave, I need to get something straight." Tucker's head shot up. *What was Mrs. Baker up to now?* "You're not engaged? Or you are engaged?"

"Not engaged," Tucker said firmly. "But we are courting. I assume that is all right with you?" He said it in mirth, but his surrogate granny's expression turned solemn.

"That depends. What are your intentions?" Everyone was silent, but suddenly she began laughing. "Go on, off you go."

Tucker expelled a huge breath and then laughed. "You had me there for a minute," he said, then stood. "Shall we?" He outstretched a hand to Maggie and helped her to her feet. Just touching her sent his nerve endings spiraling. He couldn't wait to hold her close once more, but knew it would be some time before that happened again. After all, there were rules to courtship, and Mrs. Baker would ensure he followed them.

Even if he didn't want to.

Tucker helped Maggie into her coat. "There's still a bit of a chill in the air. It's a beautiful day though, so it should soon warm up." He reveled in having her so close and couldn't wait for the day they married. The thought made him pause. *Would Maggie ever agree to marrying him?* After the experience she'd already had, he doubted it. Right now, though, he was getting ahead of himself.

Take it easy and don't scare her off. That was his plan. First, though, he had to convince her not to leave in a few days, as she'd told him she would. He could only guess that by agreeing to let him court her, she planned on staying a little longer. Of course, she was distraught when she'd agreed, so Maggie may have already changed her mind.

It was the last thing he wanted, and would have to work to make it so.

"I'll be back in time to help with the diner," Maggie called over her shoulder, and Tucker knew she would be true to her word. That gave him less than two hours with her. He would have to make the most of it.

Tucker knew he would.

"I've seen little of the town. Show me around?" He'd planned to do that, but with the short time they had available, there wasn't a lot they could do. He headed toward the main road.

"You've likely seen most of the stores, so we could visit the housing parts of town."

"Sounds good. All I've seen is Mrs. Baker's cottage, the mercantile, and the stores close to it. It will be interesting to see the rest of Grand Falls. Most towns are the same, I know, but I enjoy seeing the various styles of houses." She stared at him and grinned. Tucker wasn't sure if she was having a joke with him, or whether she was serious. He hadn't really seen that side of her, so it was refreshing.

He guided Maggie down a narrow alley way. "This is the men's boarding house," he said. "We get a lot of itinerant workers around here, and that's where they generally stay. Grand Falls has grown tremendously over the past couple of years, to the point we had to bring in additional carpenters."

They strolled past the impressive looking boarding house and headed toward the newest houses. "These houses are all relatively new. Each time a new store is added, another home is needed too. We're going to end up being a large city if we're not careful." It wasn't something Tucker particularly wanted, but it would help the livery, and also the diner. Not to mention the other stores in town.

"They are lovely. The homes in Shady Hollow are mostly older, and many are in disrepair. Only those who can afford it have kept up the maintenance."

"There's an open area close to here. Would you like to see it?" Tucker used to love playing there as a small child. It was one of the few places he and Charlie could get away from their father. It hadn't occurred to him that his mother also needed the break.

"Is it a playground?" She stared at him wide-eyed, and Tucker had no doubt she was excited by the prospect. "Shady Hollow doesn't have a playground, which was disappointing."

"I imagine it would be. What sort of childhood did you have?" He genuinely wanted to know if her childhood was a happy one. "Here we are. What do you think?"

She ran to the swing and sat on it. Tucker immediately began to push her gently. The smile on her face set his nerve endings on edge. "Oh, there's a gazebo. Can we sit in there for a bit?"

He reached for her hand and reveled in the feel of her. He tucked her arm into his, and they headed that way. This could be a wonderful opportunity to talk to Maggie about his plan. It involved her and couldn't go ahead without her, so it was imperative.

"Maggie…I need to ask you something," he said as they sat on the wooden seat. She glanced up at him, her expression wary. "It's about Mrs. Baker." The relief on her face was palpable. What did she think he was going to ask? She nodded, and he continued. "I know you want to help her. I do too. She's like a granny to me, part of the family."

"I noticed that."

It was his turn to nod. "How would you feel about taking over the diner?"

Maggie spluttered. "I…what…?" She seemed lost for words. "I had the same idea, but on pondering it over, I don't think she would like that."

Tucker was certain Maggie was right. "It would only be for a few days. A week at most – to give her a break. I'm afraid for her health. She looks ready to drop."

Maggie's face softened. "She does. It's the reason I agreed to help her out. I'd be gone from here by now otherwise." Her statement cut Tucker to his heart. He'd hope she would stay because of him. *Weren't they courting?* They couldn't do that if she up and left. "I mean…" She fidgeted with her hands. "Now that we're courting, that changes things."

He studied her and decided that was what she meant. "Could you take over the cooking for a few days?" The shock on her face worried him. "You know how to cook, right?"

Now she looked annoyed. "Of course I can cook. And I can bake. Not as good as Mrs. Baker, I'm certain, but I can get by." She pouted now, which meant she was truly irritated at him. "I've been helping with the cooking these past few days."

Relief flooded him. "That settles it then. We'll talk to Mrs. Baker about it when we return."

"I can't handle the diner by myself." She appeared truly worried.

"I know. I'm going to help you."

Maggie laughed. "What? I can do it. I'm pretty sure." Now he was hurt.

"Can you? What experience do you have?"

He rounded right back at her. "What experience do you have?" As far as Tucker was aware, Maggie had no prior experience in a diner or restaurant of any sort.

"You are quite infuriating at times, Tucker Smith. I want to go home." Maggie stood then, her frustration with him more than a little apparent.

He needed to smooth things over. The last thing he wanted was for Maggie to be angry with him. "I'm sorry. I didn't mean to upset you. I just want to help an old lady out." Tucker knew he shouldn't, but he wrapped his arms around her, and Maggie leaned into him. She felt so good in his arms. But Tucker knew he must not get used to it.

He didn't want to scare her away. Heck, she would leave town at the drop of a hat!

Then, the last thing he expected happened. She tilted her head upward and stared into his face. She licked her lips as though daring him to kiss her.

Did he want to kiss her? Without a doubt, but what would people say if they saw them? Tucker glanced about – there was no one in sight. He studied her. The last thing he wanted was to do something Maggie didn't want.

"Are you certain?" he whispered, although there was no one around to hear him.

She closed her eyes momentarily, then opened them to gaze at him. "I'm certain." He didn't ask again, but leaned down into her and kissed her luscious lips. Tucker had kissed women before, but none like Maggie. She was appealing in every way. She was refined, gentle, and someone he wanted to be around.

Her arms went up his back, and a shudder went through him. How, after only a few days, could he be so enamored with this woman? He felt drawn to her, and didn't want to let her go.

His fingers roamed up her back and into her hair. Tucker could stay like this all day, but he knew it wasn't an option. It wouldn't be long before they'd have to make their way back to the diner.

Not that they'd spent that long away from there, but he wanted to iron out all the details for the break they were giving Mrs. Baker before they returned.

He reluctantly pulled away from Maggie. He chuckled as he heard her sigh. "We will have to leave soon," he whispered. It was the last thing he wanted, but they were on a time frame.

He guided her back down to the seat of the gazebo. "We should work out the details before we return. I know Mrs. Baker will object. I'm sure you do too, but we need to be firm."

"Hmmm."

"She comes across as ruthless, but deep down, she's as gentle as a lamb."

Maggie's eyes opened wide. "Really?" she asked quietly. "Are we talking about the same person?" She chuckled then. "Because that doesn't sound like the Mrs. Baker I know."

"You could be right, but I think we should be able to convince her." Tucker rubbed a hand across his chin. "Are you confident about the cooking side of things? I can seat the customers and deliver the meals to the tables."

"Mrs. Baker has all her recipes written down, so anything I'm uncertain of, I can use that for reference."

"Right. Let's go then."

Maggie took a deep breath. Her uncertainty made Tucker have second thoughts. What if Mrs. Baker refused? What would they do then? But he knew the answer – if she refused, there was absolutely nothing they could do about it.

As they strolled back to the cottage, Maggie leaned into him. When Tucker had returned home after his awful father's death, the last thing he expected was to meet his soulmate. And he was certain he had. All he had to do now was convince Maggie he was hers.

Mrs. Baker leaned forward in the armchair, a mug of coffee in her hands. "This plan of yours – how long is it for again?"

She glared at Tucker. It was obvious his surrogate granny was convinced he was behind the idea. "A few days. A week at most."

"And I'm supposed to sit around doing nothing while you two do all the work? Not happening."

He glanced across at Maggie, hoping she could convince the old lady. "You're tired. We all know you are," Maggie said gently. "There's no reason you can't be at the diner while we do most of the work. Right, Tucker?"

He stared at her. Exactly what did that mean? "Er…"

Mrs. Baker glared at him. "Doing what exactly?"

"Well, you can see the customers to their tables. Or you can take payment as they leave."

"Yes, of course," Tucker said cautiously. He wasn't sure what he was meant to say, but it sounded like a good idea. "That way, you still get to see the people you like chatting with."

She glared at him again, but then her expression softened somewhat. "And this is supposed to happen when?"

"We can start today." Tucker felt a little more certain now, but was still a little wary. Mrs. Baker agreeing was the last thing he expected, but was pleasantly surprised that she had.

"I've already put the roast on, but that seems reasonable. Are you sure you can manage?" She looked directly at Maggie. After all, she was the one who had to do most of the work. The cooking, at least.

"I am certain I can. I know how to cook, as you already know. Serving the tables isn't that hard. I'm sure we can teach Tucker how to do it." She grinned then, and Mrs. Baker laughed.

Tucker let out the breath he didn't realize he'd been holding. He stared at her for a moment. *Had she really agreed to letting him and Maggie take over the diner for the next few days?* He shook himself mentally. No matter how good his plan was, he honestly didn't think she would agree.

But she did, and now it was up to the two of them to prove to Mrs. Baker she could take a break and not have the diner suffer as a result.

She placed her mug on the side table, then stood. She stepped over to Tucker and hugged him and then shifted to Maggie. "Thank you both," she said, her voice quite emotional. "I haven't had a break since my Henry died – over ten years ago now."

Maggie was certain she saw a tear trickle down her face, but Mrs. Baker turned away quickly, not giving her the chance to verify.

"Right, that's settled then," Tucker said, rubbing his hands together. "Maggie and I should probably leave now."

"I'm coming with you." He sighed. What was the point of them taking over the diner if Mrs. Baker went with them?

"That's a great idea," Maggie said, surprising him. "You've already begun to cook for tonight's supper, so I'll need to know where you're at."

"Tucker, you'll need to get out of that suit. It could get ruined when you help in the kitchen." Mrs. Baker was firm in her instruction. "Wear clean pants and a tidy shirt. And perhaps a vest if you have one that's suitable." She hooked her arm through Maggie's. "Maggie and I will go on ahead and get things sorted while you change. We'll meet you there."

If he didn't know better, Tucker would think he was being given the brush off.

Chapter Six

Maggie brushed the hair back off her face. She knew working in the kitchen alone would be hard work, but this was far harder than she'd expected. But she couldn't complain. She wasn't an elderly lady of seventy plus, and she hadn't been running the diner virtually alone for the last decade.

She had lived a privileged life and hadn't done a hard day's work in her life – until she came to Grand Falls, that was. Mrs. Baker had been so kind to her, Maggie owed her this much. It did, however, worry her what would happen a little further down the track.

Until Tucker came into the equation, she had no thought of staying. But things changed the moment he asked to court her. If she was honest with herself, she'd already thought about staying. It was lovely here, and she didn't really want to leave. All that said, she barely knew Tucker. *If things didn't work out with him, what would she do?*

Maggie shook herself mentally. Now was not the time to worry about such things. She had to finish making the gravy and then put the apple pie in the oven. The muffins were cooked, and the cherry cobbler still needed to be sliced ready for the desserts.

Phew! *Had she really just prepared all that food by herself?* Well, almost by herself. Mrs. Baker was sitting in the kitchen, throwing orders left and right, ensuring everything was done as it should be. A few times she tried to take over, but Tucker guided her into the diner, where he used the excuse of getting her to teach him how to set the tables ready for the onslaught of customers.

Not that he would admit it, but Maggie was certain Tucker was enjoying himself. He might not feel the same way once customers arrived, and he was running back and forth between the kitchen and the tables.

At least with Mrs. Baker there, he didn't have to worry about the payment side of things. She had decided to do that, and play hostess, at least for two or three nights until they settled. It made Maggie smile, because it meant Mrs. Baker had accepted they were giving her a break of at least a few days, and possibly more.

She slipped the apple pie into the oven, then set to work on the chicken pot pie. Pastry was not her favorite thing to make, mostly because it wasn't something she'd done much of. But Mrs. Baker was a patient teacher and showed her exactly what needed to be done to make the pastry light and crispy. Now Maggie needed to cut the chicken, dice the vegetables, and make the white sauce to cover them in.

This was fiddly since each pie had its own little dish. Maggie sighed. Mrs. Baker was meticulous about the food, and Maggie understood why. Her customers expected a certain standard, and she had to adhere to that expectation. As she cut each circle of pastry, she added it carefully to the dishes. She could get three dozen out of one batch of pastry, and according to Mrs. Baker, that was usually enough. Once it sold out, that was it for the night. There were only a handful of main dishes each night. The "chef's special" tonight was the chicken pot pie. Each night featured a different main meal, and at least three desserts. At least the latter were reasonably easy to make.

Tucker came up behind her, and Maggie sank against him. "This is hard work," she whispered.

He glanced down at her face. "Too much? I can help." She almost laughed. At his own admission, Tucker did not know how to cook.

"You are helping. What you are doing out there in the diner is necessary. I'll cope, I promise." Maggie was certain the more she did it, the easier it would become. Maybe she could change the menus around as well. But then again, Mrs. Baker may not allow her to do that.

She relaxed against Tucker, reveling in the feeling it gave her. She felt…wanted. His arms came up around her, and he kissed her cheek. "This is a good thing we're doing. I can already see Mrs. Baker relaxing. When she's not on my back, that is," he said, chuckling. "This will do her a lot of good, I'm certain of it."

Maggie shrugged out of his grip. "I need to finish these chicken pies. It won't be long and the customers will begin arriving. Are the tables ready?" She turned to face him then. Tucker looked frazzled, which was not surprising. She'd heard Mrs. Baker shouting orders about the right way to set the tables. It was only their first night taking over. Tomorrow would be better. *Wouldn't it?*

Maggie heard the bell over the entrance tinkle as she took the chicken pies out of the oven. They looked perfect. She only hoped they tasted as good as Mrs. Baker's pies. She closed her eyes and said a silent prayer. Not for her own sake, but for that of the diner's owner. The last thing Maggie wanted to do was ruin the woman's business. The Good Lord had got her through in the past, and she was certain he would be there for her today.

Tucker hurried into the kitchen, looking more frazzled than before. "Two chicken pot pies, and one roast." He looked unsure. "Or was that two roasts and one chicken pie?"

"You didn't write it down?"

He appeared confused then. "Write it down? What do you mean?"

Maggie glanced about the kitchen, then handed him a notepad and pencil. "Here, this is the order pad. If you write it down, you can't forget. Now, go back out there and apologize, and this time, put the information on the notepad." He looked relieved then and hurried back out to the dining area.

She pulled the trays down, ready to add the food once plated up. *Had she really pulled this off?* It seemed she had, but whether it passed the taste test was yet to be seen. She stirred the gravy that was keeping hot on the stove and sliced the apple pie that was now cooked, then covered it with a pile of clean kitchen towels to keep it hot – just like Mrs. Baker had shown her.

What she'd learned today was working in the kitchen was a juggling act. She would get better at it as time went on. Even over a few days, she was sure it would become easier.

Tucker returned. "Two roasts and one chicken pie." Maggie smiled, and plated up. "What can I do?"

"Take water to the table. Over there – one jug and three glasses in this case. One glass for each person." She raised her eyebrows. He might already know this, but better to know for sure than to assume and be wrong. "By the time you come back, the meals will be ready to be delivered. How busy it is out there?"

"There aren't many diners at the moment." The second the words were out of his mouth, the bell tinkled again. Before Tucker had left the kitchen, it tinkled yet again. Maggie hoped she'd made enough food to last. She'd followed Mrs. Baker's instructions regarding quantities, so they should have enough. *Shouldn't they?*

She chewed on her bottom lip, but decided there was no time to worry. Instead, she cut the desserts into portions. The muffins sat on a tray, and would be added to plates when she had a spare moment.

Tucker burst into the kitchen in a panic. "Three more tables of diners! Here are their orders." He read them out to Maggie, and she plated up while Tucker delivered water to the tables.

The bell tinkled again. When he returned, Tucker appeared even more panicked. "Take your time, and don't get overwhelmed. There's no rush," she told him gently. "Breathe." Tucker took a fortifying breath, then turned away. "Take the water and glasses with you. You'll quickly get sick of running back and forth. There's no reason you can't already have the jugs of water on the tables already."

"Now you tell me." He grinned, then disappeared again. Maggie was certain once they got into a rhythm, it would get far easier. How Mrs. Baker had managed all this time, she didn't know, but it had to stop. The woman was far too old to be running the diner alone. It's a wonder she hadn't collapsed from overwork.

"Two more chicken pies, Maggie. I hope you did plenty. They're popular."

"I made three dozen, like I was told too. I hope they taste all right." It was her biggest fear, that the food was not as good as Mrs. Baker's.

"No complaints so far," he said teasingly as he carried a pile of soiled dishes into the kitchen. "In fact, the first table has praised them. Relax, you did good." Maggie sighed with relief. The last thing she wanted was to ruin the diner's reputation. "They're ready for dessert," he said as he poured three mugs of coffee.

She added clotted cream to the requested desserts, and Tucker took them to deliver to the diners. "Tucker," she called over her shoulder. "Thank you. You're a great help. I couldn't have done this alone. I have no idea how Mrs. Tucker has done it all these years without help."

She watched as his face contorted. That usually meant Tucker was mulling over an idea. Maggie might not have known him for long, but she already understood his nuances and some of his facial expressions. "What are you thinking?" she asked quietly. *Was she worried about what he might come up with next?* If it meant helping Mrs. Baker, provided she was physically capable of it, she didn't really care.

He stared at her momentarily, then turned away. "Later," he said. "I can't discuss it now." He glanced toward Mrs. Baker, and it had Maggie wondering what he was up to. She returned to the kitchen and poured a kettle full of boiling water over the soiled dishes. They really needed a kitchen hand to do all the tedious things that wasted her time as a cook. Why Mrs. Baker hadn't done so, Maggie couldn't fathom.

She was certain it had nothing to do with money. The diner was in profit. Mrs. Baker told her so. But she also told Maggie she didn't like change, so that was likely the reason. Perhaps she could convince the elderly woman to take on a teenager to do those menial jobs. After all, it would cost her a minimum compared to an adult kitchen hand. Tucker might know someone suitable.

She filed that information to the back of her mind until she had more time to worry about it.

At the end of the evening, Maggie was exhausted. There was plenty of leftover food for the three of them to consume. Mrs. Baker looked far more relaxed tonight and was not as tired as she normally seemed. "That was a very successful exercise," she announced as they sat around the table. Maggie placed a plate of fresh biscuits in the middle of the table. They'd run out with the last meals served. Mrs. Baker's quantities worked out perfectly.

"Tonight seemed busier than normal," Maggie said questioningly.

"Only because you were cooking." Mrs. Baker chuckled, but Maggie was too tired to join in.

"Your quantities were spot on. Thank you for helping me out with those."

Mrs. Baker leaned forward, her elbows on the table. She glanced from Tucker to Maggie. "No, thank you. Both of you. I really needed a night off. I enjoyed it too. I had time to chat with everyone." A big smile cut across her face. "It was lovely."

Tucker glanced at Maggie, then reached under the table and squeezed her hand. Maggie felt the warmth flood her and was certain her cheeks had turned pink.

"How long did you say you were taking over for?" She looked excited, which Maggie didn't expect.

"A few nights? Maybe more?" She glanced across at Tucker for support.

"Even a week, if you want," he said. "Unless we both collapse from exhaustion." He laughed then, and Mrs. Baker joined in.

"You young un's. No stamina. In my day, we were far more resilient."

Maggie knew she was right. It surely didn't help she hadn't done much in the way of work until she'd arrived in Grand Falls. Suddenly the older woman turned serious. "If that's really want you both want, we can continue. Let's see how you both fare after another couple of days of running the diner. I won't interfere, but I'll be here if you need me. I'll act as hostess if you approve."

"It sounds like a grand plan," Tucker said.

Maggie nodded. "It certainly does. That way, if I need advice, you're nearby. But you can also chat with the customers."

Mrs. Baker seemed to brighten up at the last part. Maggie already knew she loved to socialize, and neither her nor Tucker wanted to take that pleasure away from her.

"Well, eat up before it goes cold," Maggie said.

She was almost too tired to eat, but knew she had two more days of this, and had to keep up her strength.

Chapter Seven

Lunch was a far easier meal to cater to. There were fewer options, and less customers. It was relatively easy. Because of that, Maggie made a couple of desserts for the evening – the sort that didn't matter if they were cold. Muffins were part of that plan.

Tucker worked in the dining room as he did the previous night, but they suggested Mrs. Baker take the time off, and surprisingly she did. It seemed strange with only the two of them there. Except for when they'd taken a stroll, that hadn't happened before. It wasn't the done thing – single women were supposed to be chaperoned. Not that Maggie had ever adhered to that rule. It really was old-fashioned.

"Two more soups please, Maggie." Tucker's voice cut into her thoughts, and Maggie turned to face him. She smiled, then filled two bowls with the thick vegetable soup. A staple item for lunchtime, she'd been told. She'd made plenty, and just as well. It seemed there were more people than Mrs. Baker told her to expect. She'd made biscuits to go with them, as well as hot bread, which was the norm.

She wasn't sure switching the menu around would please Mrs. Baker, but the diners seemed happy about it. If everything worked out with Tucker, she would be here to help Mrs. Baker, so it wouldn't be a burden for the older woman.

So far, thick vegetable soup was all that had been ordered. She had other items ready to cook if requested, such as steak, which was a favorite amongst the men. Most of the diners today were women, and they seemed content with the lighter meal.

When Tucker returned, he placed soiled dishes in the sink with the boiling water Maggie had already added there. He sidled over to her and wrapped his arms around her. "It feels good to help an old lady out, doesn't it?" His head came down, and Tucker lightly kissed her neck. Maggie knew he wouldn't do such a thing if Mrs. Baker had been around. He wouldn't risk being caught. Not that she was complaining.

"It does," she whispered, and held onto his arms. She didn't want him to let go. It felt so good. But she had work to do. They both had work to do. *What was she thinking, allowing Tucker to distract her like this?* She shrugged out of his arms and began washing dishes. Tucker picked up a kitchen cloth to help her. "I'm fine. You make sure the diner's are all okay and don't need assistance." He looked disappointed, but Maggie couldn't help that. They were here to do a specific job, and he was very distracting. She couldn't allow it.

Balancing everything in the kitchen was difficult. She couldn't fathom how Mrs. Baker had done it for so long, but realized it was probably from habit. Maggie still had to get into the rhythm of doing many things at once. At least lunch was a far easier meal, and it would soon be over.

She dried her hands and checked the roast that was cooking in the oven for this evening's meals. Every night, there was a roast of some sort. She wondered if that was necessarily a good thing. Maggie thought back to the diner in Shady Hollow. What did they serve? She was convinced they didn't have roast every day.

She shook herself. Right now, there was no time for contemplating changes. Besides, Mrs. Baker would be back at the helm in a day or two. Four at most, depending on whether they could convince her to take extra time off.

With the dishes washed and dried, and put away, Maggie concentrated her efforts back on the food. She had custard sitting on the warmer, along with the soup. She gave each of them a stir. The apple pie was not long out of the oven and was still warm. Custard was a recent addition, instead of clotted cream. She was yet to see if the diners liked that change. She would add a dollop of cream to the side, so they wouldn't miss out entirely.

"Three apple pies with custard," Tucker said as he entered the kitchen again, his arms opened wide.

"Nope, not happening," Maggie said firmly. "There is no time for that nonsense."

Now he looked hurt. "Nonsense? Holding my girl is not nonsense." He pouted then, and Maggie wasn't sure if he was serious or was teasing her. Suddenly, he began laughing. She nudged his shoulder.

"Here's the pie. Get out of here – you are far too distracting." He did as he was told, but it left an emptiness that Maggie couldn't understand. After all, she knew Tucker would be back shortly with the next round of orders.

She flopped against the counter. She wasn't exactly tired, but took the opportunity to rest before the next order came in, and she had to plate up. She had just finished making another batch of biscuits when Tucker returned. "I think that's it. The diner is empty, and I have you all to myself." He smirked then, and Maggie wanted to wipe it from his handsome face.

He stepped toward her, but froze when the bell over the door tinkled. "You didn't lock the door?" Maggie asked, feeling quite disappointed at the interruption.

"Where is everyone?" Mrs. Baker's voice rang through the empty dining room.

"In the kitchen," Maggie called out as she heard the click of the lock. Mrs. Baker had ensured they had no stragglers in the diner.

She heard footsteps, then they were joined by the diner's owner. "How did it go today?"

Maggie glanced into the large pot that held the soup. "Very well. There's enough left for the three of us to have lunch, but not a lot more."

"There was a steady stream of customers, and it kept us busy," Tucker said. He headed to the till, and handed over the takings to Mrs. Baker, who had followed behind.

She pushed his hands away. "Hang on to that for supplies," she said. "Or put them on the diner's account at the mercantile. Whatever works for you. I have an account at the butcher's as well."

"I…" Maggie wasn't sure what to say." *Was Mrs. Baker giving up?* Maggie hoped not. It was not her intention, or that of Tucker, to push the store owner out. They wanted to give her a short break.

"You know this is only temporary, right?" Tucker said firmly. He'd known Mrs. Baker far longer than Maggie, so she would let him deal with her. "You were looking tired and stressed. A few days and you'll be good as new." He stepped toward her and pulled the older woman into his arms. "You're like a grandmother to me, and I hate to see you so stressed."

"I know," she said, a tear rolling down her cheek. "But I'm tired." She glanced up at Tucker, who towered over her far more than he did over Maggie. "I don't know if I can keep doing this much longer."

Did she mean taking a break or running the diner? Maggie was confused.

"I have a plan of my own, only I need to think it through a bit longer. Can you bear with an old lady for a few more days?"

Maggie glanced across at Tucker. He was staring across at her. *What did this mean for the two of them?* Providing what she thought Mrs. Baker was hinting at was what they were both thinking she meant.

"Do you mind if I employ a teenager to help in the kitchen? With dishes and other menial tasks?"

Mrs. Baker pushed away from Tucker. "Of course. Anything you want. I see you've already changed the menu somewhat." She raised her eyebrows, her lips puckered. But then she chuckled. "Honestly, I don't care. Whatever works for you works for me. The menu was getting tired anyway – I should have changed it a long time ago."

"I'm certain there must be someone who would like the work," Tucker said. "Let me think about it. Unless you know someone, Mrs. Baker."

She raised her eyebrows again. "I'm surprised you don't call me granny," she said, then laughed. It lightened the mood, and for that, Maggie was grateful. "I'm going now. I'll see you soon, Maggie?"

She was gone before Maggie had a chance to answer.

Left alone in the diner again, Maggie stared across at Tucker. They'd both near collapsed at the table after Mrs. Baker left. "I wonder what she has in mind," he finally said.

Maggie was wondering the same thing. "I'm uncertain, but you don't think she's retiring, do you?" Surely not. The woman was an institution in Grand Falls. She'd owned the diner for as long as most people could remember. The last thing Maggie wanted was to push the dear woman out of her own business. Unless, of course, that was what she wanted.

But was it what Maggie wanted? She wasn't sure she wanted to take it over. It wasn't something she'd thought about until now. Because until a few minutes ago, it wasn't on the table, and wasn't even an option.

Maggie stood and went to the kitchen, returning with two mugs of coffee. "We have some thinking to do," she said firmly.

"Our idea backfired," Tucker said, his expression sad. "I didn't mean to make her feel she was being pushed out." He hung his head low, and Maggie knew he was quite upset about what they'd caused.

She reached across the table and placed her hand over his. Tucker's head shot up. "I don't think that is the case at all," she told him gently. "What I believe is Mrs. Baker has realized that the diner can successfully run without her, and she doesn't need to almost kill herself for it to continue."

"Could we do it?" His voice was low, little more than a whisper. "Charlie can run the livery on his own, so that's not an issue. Do you think we could run the diner alone?"

She glanced across the table at him, then closed her eyes for about thirty seconds. "No. Not alone. We'd need help, just like Mrs. Baker would need help if she continued." Maggie let out a long breath. She felt better for verbalizing what she'd been thinking for the past minutes that had seemed like hours. The entire time Mrs. Baker talked about her plan, Maggie felt she knew what was coming. The fact she needed to sleep during the day should have been a clue, but Maggie missed it.

The woman was in her seventies, for goodness' sake. How had she kept going except for her strong belief in God and the Church? Maggie figured she would never know. But perhaps her own arrival in Grand Falls had been the catalyst for Mrs. Baker's decision, if indeed that was what she was planning.

Maggie took a sip of her coffee. She needed to make some decisions of her own. She couldn't continue to live with Mrs. Baker, especially if she took over the running of the kitchen on a regular basis. She would have to commit to staying in Grand Falls or leaving. She couldn't continue on this uncertain route as she'd been doing.

Tucker stared at her. "What are you thinking?"

He had to be as confused as Maggie, but he wasn't giving anything away, either. "I have to make some decisions. If Mrs. Baker is giving up the diner, we would have to be paid a wage. It's obvious from the takings for lunch alone, that's possible, but would she want to part with that much money? Not to mention the help we'd need to secure."

"It's a lot to think about for sure." Tucker threw back the rest of his coffee and stood. "I need to get these tables sorted before supper. Do you need any help in the kitchen?"

"Dishes," she said, then swallowed down the last of her coffee and hurried into the kitchen, the weight of the world on her shoulders.

Chapter Eight

Tucker headed toward the Apothecary. He wasn't sure what sort of reaction he would get there. It had been a while since he'd had anything to do with the Ambrewster family, and heard Johnny was working there as an apprentice. He was a smart kid and deserved a break.

He opened the door and saw the boy's head pop up from behind the counter as he stepped inside. Tucker took a second look. "Johnny?" No longer a boy, he was a man now.

"Tucker? When did you arrive back in town?"

He shrugged his shoulders, trying to loosen them. Tucker did not know why he felt so stressed coming here. Johnny was an old friend. Well, not a friend exactly. He was the brother of an old girlfriend. It wasn't exactly the same thing. "I came to ask about your sister."

"Which one?" He squinted at Tucker then. "Oh. Callie."

Callie was a little younger than Tucker, and he'd courted her for a short time. There was far too much going on in his own turbulent life, and they parted ways. He'd left town not long after that. "Yes, Callie. Is she still around?"

Johnny glared at him then. "She's back in town, if that's what you mean. Ma convinced her to come home after her husband died."

"Husband?" Why hadn't he thought it a possibility? They were both of a marrying age, so he should have realized. "I'm sorry – I didn't know." He was tempted to turn around and leave right then, but the need was great. "I…I wondered if she needed a job."

"She's not working at the livery." He turned his back on Tucker then, disgust rolling off his tongue. A man looking out for his sister. More likely than not, she was still in mourning.

"Not the livery. I've been helping Mrs. Baker at the diner, along with Maggie Coulter. We need a kitchen hand."

Johnny spun around to face him again. He straightened his tie and thought carefully before responding. "That might be a possibility. Give me the details, and I'll talk to her tonight when I get home."

"Mrs. Baker is taking a break. Maggie and I, we need help. I thought Callie…"

"I'll talk to her," Johnny said firmly, then went back to what he'd been doing. Tucker was effectively dismissed and left the store.

He stood outside, peering in. For only a moment. He'd lost Callie because of his father's violence, and he didn't blame her. But leaving town soon after was unforgiveable. Even if he did so at his mother's insistence. She was trying to save him, knew he would one day retaliate and possibly kill the old man. It was a wonder Charlie hadn't done so.

Tucker shook his head and walked away. The last thing he needed was to revisit old wounds. He was happy now the old man was gone, but he would live with those regrets for the rest of his life.

He strolled into the diner, to the clatter of pots and pans in the kitchen. Maggie was already in full swing. "I'm back," he called, not wanting to startle her.

"I'm in here," she answered, as if he did not know where she was. The thought made him chuckle. "Well?" she asked when he reached the kitchen.

"Johnny will ask his sister tonight." He finally took in what he'd been told. "She's a year younger than me, and a widow." He was genuinely sad for her and wondered what her life had been like. He was certain her mother would be happy she was home.

She was getting on, and no longer able to cope on her own. She'd always been kind to Tucker, knowing about his family situation. Their home was like a refuge to him, and it was the reason he'd got to know Callie as well as he did.

He shook himself mentally. It was water under the bridge now, and he needed to move on. Deep down, though, he wanted to know that she'd been treated well, that Callie's husband had been a good person. She'd known his situation; surely she wouldn't let herself get dragged into a similar position?

Maggie handed him a coffee, and Tucker gladly took it. "What can I do to help?"

"Sit down and take a break. You look completely done in." She studied him then, and it was unnerving. She was trying to read him, to understand every part of him, but it was the last thing he wanted.

"We were friends." He glanced up at her then. It wasn't quite true. "We courted," he said slightly above a whisper. "I didn't think for one minute she'd be a widow at her age."

"Children?"

His head shot up. "What?" It was a possibility, he supposed, but not something he'd even considered. He took a huge mouthful of coffee. "I have no idea. I didn't think to ask."

"It might make things difficult for her if children are involved." He hadn't thought of that possibility either.

He nodded, not willing to contemplate that scenario. His Callie, all grown up and a mother. It made him feel old, and brought home the fact he should have been married by now, but because of his father, Tucker had put it on hold. What if he was like his old man? He shook the thought away. He'd not been violent, even once in his life. Except for the time he'd retaliated again his father. That's when his mother sent him away, worried for his safety.

The knocking at the diner's door brought Tucker out of his thoughts. When he glanced up, Mrs. Baker stood at the door, peering in. "Can't get into my own diner," she mumbled when he unlocked the door. "Just came to see if you needed help." Maggie handed her a mug of coffee as she sat down. "Did you get yourselves a kitchen hand yet?"

"Did you know Callie was back in town?" Tucker asked.

Mrs. Baker became suddenly solemn. "I did. Terrible situation." She took a sip of coffee, then sat back and crossed her arms. It was clear any information would not be easily forthcoming. Tucker was going to have to pry it out of her.

"Her brother told me she's a widow."

"She is." She took another sip of coffee. "Any muffins ready yet?"

Maggie laughed. They both knew Mrs. Baker loved muffins. Maggie headed toward the kitchen, returning with a plate of freshly baked orange muffins. The older woman reached for a muffin, breaking it up and taking a small bite, savoring the flavor. "You did good."

Maggie smiled. She was using Mrs. Baker's recipes, per the old lady's instructions, so how could she go wrong? Tucker wondered if they would be privy to the diner owner's *plan* today, or whether she intended to string them along a little longer.

"What's on tonight's menu?" Her words were out of the blue, and Maggie stuttered, but only for a moment.

"I, er, pot roast, roast chicken, and beef stew. I haven't worked out the desserts yet, but I was about to when you arrived."

Mrs. Baker studied her. "Always have your menus planned at least a day ahead. I've always had them planned a week early. The mercantile doesn't always have stock. That way, they have time to get supplies in for you."

Tucker watched as Mrs. Baker spoke. Something wasn't right here, but he couldn't put his finger on it. Since when did she give away trade secrets? And then it hit him. She wasn't planning on taking a break, she was giving up working at the diner. It was the reason she'd told them to hire whoever they needed.

Was her plan to have the two of them running and managing the business for her? Tucker wasn't sure it was something he wanted to do long term, but despite being run off his feet at meal times, he couldn't say he was unhappy with his new temporary line of work. The question was, could or would he be happy to do it long term?

"What's going on?" he asked quietly.

She stared at him, then glared. It was as though she'd suddenly realized he knew what she was up to. "I don't know what you mean," she said, then puckered her lips. Oh, she was up to something all right, and Tucker was positive he knew what it was. He'd known Mrs. Baker for far too long, and understood her moods and her expressions, just as she knew and understood his.

He reached across the table and covered her hand. "It's me, Tucker. You can tell me anything."

A slow smile crossed her face. It was the expression she used when she was concocting something. She could be a cunning old lady when she wanted to, and that was often. She suddenly glanced across the table at Maggie. "Think you could stay a little longer? I need a bit more of a break."

Maggie resisted the urge to sigh, then smiled. "Sure. I can do that. I'll look for alternative accommodation."

"Don't do that," Mrs. Baker said, reaching out to hold her hand. "I'm enjoying your company."

"As long as you're sure?"

"I'm certain. So that's organized, and I'm off as soon as I finish this delicious muffin."

Maggie glanced across the table at him, confusion on her face. Tucker shrugged. He was convinced there was still something going on. He just couldn't fathom what it was.

Heading back into the kitchen, Maggie leaned in and kissed Mrs. Baker on the cheek. "Thank you," she said, then disappeared into her new domain. Soon pots and pans were rattling, and he heard humming. What began as a stressful situation for Maggie had turned into something far more than either of them imagined. She had found her place right here in Grand Falls, but especially here in the diner. Mrs. Baker had done that for her – taken Maggie under her wing. *Is this what the old lady planned from the beginning?*

Tucker had thought this was all his and Maggie's idea, but now he was beginning to wonder.

Callie wandered into the diner around ten the next morning. Maggie was in the midst of preparing for the lunch rush when she arrived.

"Maggie, this is Callie." The two women nodded toward each other, and Callie glanced about.

"My brother told me you might have work for me." She continued to gaze around the kitchen. "What would that involve? I can cook, if you need help in that area."

Maggie studied her. "Nothing so *glamorous,* I'm afraid. I need a kitchen hand, but since you can cook, you can probably help when it's needed. That is, if you want to."

They chatted about the duties she would be expected to perform, and Callie added in a few things she would be happy to carry out as well. That included waiting tables and setting up when needed. It was a relief, as Maggie wasn't sure how pliable Callie would be in that regard. But it sounded as though she was happy to help out in any way necessary.

"When can you start?" she asked. She hadn't even discussed wages with the woman.

Callie appeared startled. "I…well, right now if you want me to." Maggie smiled.

"Let's talk money first, then you can decide."

Callie waved her words away. "Let's get to work. I'm sure the pay is acceptable." She leaned closer to Maggie. "I don't enjoy talking about money." Then she strolled casually into the kitchen and started work on the dishes sitting in the sink.

The lunch rush had begun. Maggie made even more soup for this service since they'd almost run out last time. She also made a dozen extra biscuits and made bread rolls instead of loaves of bread. It all went down well. Despite her best efforts, little of the other menu items were ordered. It got her to wondering if only having soup on the lunch menu would work. But she knew Mrs. Baker wouldn't agree to it. Perhaps another type of soup? Pumpkin perhaps? That would give the diners a choice, without having to prepare other menu items that may be wasted. It seemed like a good idea to Maggie. Now all she had to do was run it past Mrs. Baker. Then again, the diner owner had hinted that it was her decision while she ran the kitchen.

Hmmm, she would think about it.

"Mrs. Baker is out in the dining room," Tucker said as he rushed in. "She's ordered a meal. What do I do?"

Maggie stared at him. "What do you mean? We serve her. She's likely testing us."

"Of course she is," Tucker growled. He told Maggie the order, and she plated it up.

"Might I take it to her?" Callie suggested. "I haven't seen Mrs. Baker for a very long time." Maggie watched as Callie carried the meal into the dining room, then sat down next to their *customer* and chatted. They looked like old friends, and of course, that's exactly what they were.

Already Maggie had found her new kitchen hand to be good value. An added bonus was she knew most people in town, if not all. That could be a tremendous help. Especially to Maggie, who knew few people.

Unable to stand idly by any longer, Maggie stirred the soup. The last thing she needed was for the soup to burn. She removed an apple cobbler from the oven and placed the last tray of biscuits in it. The aroma in her kitchen was amazing.

That thought made Maggie pause. It wasn't her kitchen, it belonged to Mrs. Baker, and she would be back in a matter of days, if not sooner. Her life would be far easier with the addition of Callie, as Maggie's load had already been lightened.

She cut the cobbler and placed the slices into bowls. She then covered them with a thickly folded table cloth, to keep the heat in. Stirring the custard, Maggie contemplated what she would do once Mrs.

Baker was back where she belonged – right there in this kitchen.

If she was honest with herself, she had no idea what her future held. With no job, she would likely have to move on. It was far too soon for Tucker to propose, if he even had that on his mind. Courting didn't necessarily mean he wanted to marry her, only that he wanted to get to know her better.

"Three apple cobblers with custard," Tucker said as he entered the kitchen. He placed the soiled dishes on the edge of the sink and Callie immediately began to wash them. She was certainly an asset to the diner. The kitchen hadn't been cleaner since before she arrived. The moment a pot was finished with, she scrubbed it. Everything was put back where it belonged in record time. All countertops were scrubbed clean and wiped down constantly, and she helped Tucker do the same with the tables.

"I wish you would slow down," she told Callie. The woman looked startled.

"You don't want me to clean?" She seemed a little upset.

"I don't want you to kill yourself with overwork. That's exactly what Mrs. Baker has been doing. There's no rush. Take your time. Please."

Tucker raised his eyebrows at her. *Was she overreacting?* Maggie didn't think so, but perhaps she was. She was on edge about her future, and unsure about having Mrs. Baker as a customer.

The moment she finished plating up the desserts, she handed them to Tucker, who quickly left. Then she pulled down mugs, ready for the coffee orders she knew would follow. "I'm sorry," she said, turning to Callie. I'm worried about what Mrs. Baker thinks of my cooking."

"It's all right. I understand." She smiled then, and Maggie was relieved. The last thing she wanted to do was upset her new kitchen hand. She was already a godsend, and Maggie did not know how she had coped without her.

"We've been summoned." Tucker's words cut through her heart. Did Mrs. Baker hate her food? Maggie's heart pounded, and she was certain her legs would collapse underneath her.

Maggie followed Tucker out into the dining room. Mrs. Baker was sitting at the best table in the diner, according to Tucker's comment to his mother the night they'd dined there.

"Sit, both of you," she said, glancing around the diner. "We need to talk."

She hated the food, Maggie was certain of it. "I'm sorry. I'll do better," Maggie said, her voice breaking.

"My dear girl," Mrs. Baker almost shouted. "The food is amazing. I need to talk to you both, but in private. Will you both be available at, say, four this afternoon?"

Maggie glanced at Tucker, who glanced at her. Mrs. Baker certainly knew how to get them on edge, and wondering.

"Of course," they both said in unison.

"Here, in the diner?" Tucker asked.

"Yes," Mrs. Baker said, then lifted her mug and sipped her coffee. "Make sure there are plenty of muffins. I'm bringing a guest." Then she motioned for them to leave her alone.

Maggie returned to the kitchen, filled with confusion. Perhaps this meeting would answer all her questions. *But what if it meant leaving Tucker and Grand Falls?* She wasn't sure it was an option she wanted to even contemplate.

Chapter Nine

The closer it got to four, the more nervous Maggie became. Tucker was nervous too. He sauntered into the kitchen. "Everything ready?" He leaned in to take in the aroma of the blueberry muffins that came out of the oven just moments ago.

Then he checked the kettle to ensure there was enough water in it. He pulled down the mugs and laid them out, ready for the coffees when needed. He simply couldn't help himself – he pottered about trying to fill in time.

"For goodness' sakes, Tucker. Can you please leave my kitchen?" He was hurt. He was simply trying to help.

No, that wasn't true. He was every bit as nervous as Maggie and needed to do something. Anything, provided it took his mind off the upcoming meeting. He worried Mrs. Baker wanted to come back early. She needed this break, and he wanted to spend the time with Maggie. They had really begun to know each other.

Oh, how selfish that sounded! Mrs. Baker was his priority, of course. At her age, the older woman should be taking it easy, not running about cooking for her customers. At the very least, having Callie to help would make a big difference to her workload. He mentally shook himself. He didn't know what was in store for them, and his best guess wasn't going to help. He had to push his impatience aside and wait for the big announcement.

He glanced up as the bell over the diner door tinkled. True to her word, Mrs. Baker had a guest. Tucker knew this man, but couldn't recall who he was. His mind was a ball of fuzz right now. It would come to him, he was certain, but probably too late to matter.

The pair headed toward Mrs. Baker's favorite table up the back of the diner. With Callie there, it was the only place that ensured complete privacy, so he completely understood. He waved and was acknowledged with a nod, but they continued on their way.

Tucker stuck his head around the kitchen door. "They're here," he told Maggie, and she thrust a tray of coffee filled mugs, cream, and sugar into his hands. She carried a plate full of muffins.

"After you," he said, ushering her forward.

"I wonder what it's about," she whispered, before hurrying to the table.

"Thank you both for making yourselves available," Mrs. Baker said. "The muffins smell delicious, Maggie."

Tucker wanted to dispense with the niceties and get on with it, whatever 'it' was. His heart was pounding, and he was developing a headache.

"Let me introduce you to Mr. Abraham Carstairs, my lawyer."

Lawyer? Was she planning on suing them for taking over the diner while she had a break? Surely not, but then again…

"Mr. Carstairs has drawn up the papers, but I need for you both to agree. Otherwise, it simply won't work."

Tucker was more confused than ever. "What won't work?"

Maggie stared first at Mrs. Baker, then at Tucker. She looked as confused as he felt.

"You're a clever man. Surely you've worked it out by now?" Mrs. Baker reached for a muffin, then offered one to her guest. He complied. "I'll let Mr. Carstairs explain." Her voice sounded as though it was breaking up. Had she been enticed to do something she didn't want to do?

The lawyer cleared his throat. "Mrs. Baker secured my services to draw up this paperwork. I have to be sure you are both in agreement, and if so, your signatures in the affirmative will be binding."

"It has to be both of you. All or none," Mrs. Baker added. She turned to Mr. Carstairs again. "Go on, tell them. The suspense is killing me."

"Mrs. Baker has decided to retire." Tucker guessed as much. But why had she employed a lawyer? "She is requesting the two of you take over the business. At a price." Tucker knew the price would be far too high for either of them to afford. "There's also a condition."

His heart raced. Mrs. Baker always wanted to get her own way. Usually she did. "What is the condition?" he asked warily. He watched as Maggie closed her eyes, distress showing on her lovely face.

Mrs. Baker waved her hands in front of herself, indicating he need not worry about it. He trusted her, so did as he was told.

Mr. Carstairs opened his mouth to speak, but Mrs. Baker again motioned, this time, for him to stop talking. "Do you have five dollars on you, Tucker?"

He was confused, but reached for his wallet. Pulling out five dollars, he handed it over.

"And you, Maggie?"

"I, er, I think so, but I'll have to get my reticule to be certain."

"Go on then. Run. I don't have all day."

Maggie stood, then hurried to the kitchen where her reticule was stored. When she returned, Maggie had four dollars in her hands. Mrs. Baker stared at her in dismay. "Do you have another dollar, Tucker? Hurry up; I don't have all day."

That was the Mrs. Baker he knew. The one who demanded perfection. He reached into his wallet again and handed over the last dollar. She turned to Maggie then. "You must pay Tucker back that dollar. Promise me."

"She doesn't n…"

"Promise me," she demanded.

Tucker was more confused than ever. "I will," Maggie said. "I promise."

Mrs. Baker's lawyer pushed two documents forward. One for Maggie and one for Tucker. "Please sign these papers. You sign here Miss Coulter, and you here Mr. Smith."

Tucker looked over the paperwork. His eyes opened in amazement. "This can't be right," he said, glancing up to face Mrs. Baker.

"It's right, my boy. Now sign." Again, Tucker did as instructed and Maggie followed suit. "Now all you have to do is agree to marry this young lady."

Tucker almost sputtered – he was so lost for words. "What?" Not that he objected to marrying Maggie. He'd fallen in love her over these last weeks they'd spent together. It wouldn't be a burden. Whether Maggie agreed was another thing entirely.

Tucker pulled himself together as best he could. "I'm guessing that is the condition you failed to disclose," he said, his voice as steady as he could manage.

Abraham Carstairs stood. "Congratulations. You two are the new owners of the *Grand Falls Diner*." He then returned all his papers to his briefcase and left without another word.

"When is the wedding?" Mrs. Baker demanded. "I want an invitation." She tried to hold back a smile, but failed dismally, then also left.

Tucker turned to Maggie. "I'm lost for words," he near-whispered. "I want you to know I don't need a condition on a contract to marry you."

"I don't need a contract either," Maggie replied. "It didn't take long for me to fall in love with you." Her words warmed his heart.

He reached out and took her hand, then moved closer. "Just so you know, there is no such condition written on the contract."

After returning to the kitchen, which was now *her* domain, Maggie leaned against the countertop and contemplated what had occurred. "Is everything all right?" Callie asked gently.

Maggie glanced across at her. "I think so. It seems Tucker and I now own the diner." It occurred to her then why Mrs. Baker was so determined Maggie should pay Tucker back that measly dollar. She would go to the bank shortly. She now had no cash whatsoever and needed to replenish it. She suddenly had another thought and strolled over to the kitchen doorway. She watched as he appeared glued to the spot. It seemed Tucker was still in shock, as she was. "Tucker," she called out. His head shot up and he made his way toward her. "We need to change the diner's accounts into our name. We should pay for whatever is owing and start afresh."

"I agree. I have time to go there now, if you don't need me."

She had no need for his assistance, now that she had a kitchen hand. Callie was more than she could have ever dreamed of. "Oh." Another thought entered her head. Maggie decided she needed to write some of these ideas down, so she couldn't forget.

"Callie," she said gently, and the other woman turned to face her. She looked concerned. "I want to reassure you that you still have a job here. I don't know what we ever did without you."

Stepping forward, Callie dried her hands on her apron, then hugged Maggie. "Thank you," she whispered. "I must admit to being worried about it."

"Then don't. Now I need to get to work on this evening's meals." She turned back to the stove and stirred the stew. Then wiped away the tears that were streaming down her face.

"I can't believe it." Tucker sounded annoyed. Angry even. "All the accounts have been paid in full. There is not so much as a dollar outstanding."

"The least we could have done is pay the balances the diner owned." Maggie felt she owed Mrs. Baker far more than she'd given. All she had done was befriend a lonely old lady, and help her out in her hour of need.

In return, Maggie's life had changed for the better.

Mrs. Baker sat at the back of the church wearing her best outfit. Tucker turned to face his bride-to-be and caught the wide smile on the old woman's face. She'd visited the diner several times, even collected payment for them some nights.

It was obvious she was lonely, even more than before now that she wasn't working in the diner. Maggie had agreed with him to allow Mrs. Baker to become their sometime hostess – whenever Mrs. Baker pleased. She refused payment, but enjoyed wandering around the dining room, chatting with people she'd known for a very long time. It made his heart sing, knowing the old woman, who was as much family as his own mother, would live out her days happy and content. Not to mention doing whatever she wanted to do.

The organ music began, and his beautiful Maggie walked down the aisle on the arm of her father. Her parents had forgiven her for leaving the way she did, and with the passage of time, understood why she'd run.

He stared as her father patted her hand and whispered something in her ear. Tucker could only think he was asking her to reassure him of her decision. As she arrived at the altar, Tucker reached out and took her hand. His wonderful Maggie would soon be his wife. He listened carefully to the words the preacher said, waiting for those important words he longed to hear.

Preacher Devon closed his Bible and said, "I now pronounce you man and wife." Tucker's heart thudded, and he kissed Maggie like he'd never kissed her before, then led her outside where friends and family threw rice and flower petals their way.

Tucker couldn't wait to spend the rest of his life with his soulmate.

Epilogue

Twelve months later…

Maggie sat at the back of the diner breastfeeding her daughter. There was plenty of time before any customers arrived, and she wanted to see how things were running without her there. Callie had been a perfect choice as kitchen hand, but she was far more than that – she was now completely in charge, and they'd had to find a kitchen hand for her.

The teenager they'd hired seemed reliable so far, and was still young enough to learn the ways of the diner, rather than come with her own set ways of doing things.

"How is it going?" Tucker asked as he approached the pair. Maggie took the baby from her breast, and baby Esther let out an almighty scream. "Let me," he said. "You look like you could use a break."

He placed the diaper on his shoulder, then the baby, tenderly patting her back. Maggie stood back and smiled. "That's not going to work," she said firmly. "You need to pat her more strongly than that, or she won't get rid of the unwanted air."

"I know that," he said, then did as instructed. Maggie glanced across to the front door of the diner as she heard knocking.

Mrs. Baker stood outside, waiting impatiently to enter. Maggie rushed over. "I heard you were here with the baby," she said as she smiled. "I haven't had my dose of sweetness today."

Maggie locked the door behind her, then rushed into the kitchen to get her friend a coffee and a freshly baked muffin. When she returned, the baby was on Mrs. Baker's shoulder. "Your husband does not know how to burp a baby," she scolded. "You need to teach him."

Maggie laughed. "Believe me, I've tried." She took the baby so her friend could consume her afternoon tea.

"These muffins are delicious. Yours or Callie's?"

"Definitely Callie's. She is a far better cook than I'll ever be. Besides, when would I have time to bake with a small baby?" She put Esther on the other breast and sat down at the table.

"Wait until you have five or six. Or maybe more?" Mrs. Baker prodded. Maggie knew Esther had become the older woman's surrogate grandchild. After having no children of her own, she had adopted little Esther as her own. Maggie and Tucker didn't mind one bit.

After all, without her, they wouldn't be married, wouldn't own the diner, and they certainly wouldn't be living the happy contented lives they were living right now.

Maggie was convinced God was looking down at her the day she was to marry Marcus, and approved of her decision to flee. His plan for her future was mapped out, and Tucker was her soulmate, her happy ever after. She wouldn't have it any other way.

From the Author

Thank you for reading *Maggie*! I hope you enjoyed *Maggie and Tucker's* story as much as I enjoyed writing it. The *Brides of Montana* series continues with *Callie*.

Books in this series are as follows:

Emily

Grace

Victoria

Maggie

Callie

Olivia

To find out about new books, sign up for my newsletter at:

cheryl-wright.com/newsletter/

About the Author

Multi-published, award-winning and bestselling author Cheryl Wright, former secretary, debt collector, account manager, writing coach, and shopping tour hostess, loves reading.

She writes both historical and contemporary western romance, as well as romantic suspense.

She lives in Melbourne, Australia, and is married with two adult children and has six grandchildren. When she's not writing, she can be found in her craft room making greeting cards.

Links

Website: *http://www.cheryl-wright.com/*

Facebook Reader Group:
https://www.facebook.com/groups/cherylwrightauthor/

Join My Newsletter:

https://cheryl-wright.com/newsletter/

www.ingramcontent.com/pod-product-compliance
Lightning Source LLC
Chambersburg PA
CBHW070622120726
47909CB00004B/1288